Dornford Yates is the pseudonym of Cecil William Mercer. Born into a middle-class Victorian family, his parents scraped together enough money to send him to Harrow. The son of a solicitor, he qualified for the Bar but gave up legal work in favour of his great passion for writing. As a consequence of education and experience, Yates' books feature the genteel life, a nostalgic glimpse at Edwardian decadence and a number of swindling solicitors. In his heyday and as a testament to the fine writing in his novels, Dornford Yates' work was placed in the bestseller list. Indeed, 'Berry' is one of the great comic creations of twentieth-century fiction, and 'Chandos' titles were successfully adapted for television.

Finding the English climate utterly unbearable, Yates chose to live in the French Pyrénées for eighteen years before moving on to Rhodesia where he died in 1960.

ADÈLE AND CO.
AND BERRY CAME TOO
AS BERRY AND I WERE SAYING
B-BERRY AND I LOOK BACK
BERRY AND CO.
THE BERRY SCENE
BLIND CORNER
THE BROTHER OF DAPHNE
COST PRICE
THE COURTS OF IDLENESS
AN EYE FOR A TOOTH
FIRE BELOW
GALE WARNING
THE HOUSE THAT BERRY BUILT
JONAH AND CO.
NE'ER-DO-WELL
PERISHABLE GOODS
RED IN THE MORNING
SHE FELL AMONG THIEVES
SHE PAINTED HER FACE

DORNFORD YATES

BLOOD ROYAL

HOUSE OF
STRATUS

This edition published in 2001 by House of Stratus, an imprint of Stratus Books Ltd, 21 Beeching Park, Kelly Bray, Cornwall, PL17 8QS, UK.

www.houseofstratus.com

Typeset, printed and bound by House of Stratus.

A catalogue record for this book is available from the British Library and the Library of Congress.

ISBN 1-84232-968-5

To
OXFORD,
as I remember it, when I had the honour
to wear a commoner's gown

Contents

1

We Fish in Troubled Waters

No sooner had George Hanbury and I decided to visit Austria in the summer of 192– than I began to wonder what our stay in that land would bring forth. This, I think, was natural; for, though we had been there but twice, we had each time been party to matters of life and death, and, indeed, our fortunes seemed to be so bound to that handsome country that I felt I had agreed not so much to revisit a region as to re-enter an arena.

The reason for our decision was simple, namely, to put to the touch the knowledge which we had acquired of the German tongue, and, though we could have done this as well in Baden or Saxony, we naturally inclined to a district we knew and liked.

It may seem strange that two young men of leisure, not given at all to study but rather to minding their acres and hunting five days a week, should have hired a tutor to make their evenings a burden for the best part of eighteen months; but upon the two visits I have mentioned our ignorance had been the source of so much embarrassment and peril that, late in the day as it was, we determined to master German at any cost.

That we were most happy in our tutor there can be no doubt. He was an Austrian and, though he never said so, plainly of high degree. He was learned, courteous and understanding, and I can think of no company which his presence would not have improved. Of Maintenance, our home in Wiltshire, he grew, I think, very fond and, since he was so pleasant in his ways, I am sure we should never have dismissed him, but one May morning he suddenly took his leave.

"You need me no more," he said quietly, "and I must go. I have much to thank you for."

This abrupt declaration took us aback, but, when it was plain that he had made up his mind, we begged him to wait for a fortnight and go to his country with us.

He thanked us and shook his head.

"I have business," he said, "to which I must go at once: and, though our ways are the same, I do not think we shall meet."

With that, he spoke of our kindness in terms which it did not deserve and, promising to send an address to which we might write, asked that a groom might drive him to catch a train to London which left at midday.

It seemed best to argue no more, and so we parted; and that was the singular end of a relation which I am glad to think I always valued.

Fifteen days later we left for Austria by road. Bell and Rowley, our servants, went with us, and, although George Hanbury did not know it, we carried arms. We took no chauffeur because we had none to take, for we always drove and cared for the car ourselves; but we had taught the servants how a Rolls-Royce should be handled and the general attention it deserved, and no chauffeur that I have known was ever so jealous of his charge.

Bell and Rowley were ex-soldiers – quiet, steady men who knew no fear. They were most able and trusty, did with goodwill all manner of duty which no mere bodyservant could well have been desired to essay and seemed content with their lot. To their unswerving devotion this tale will testify.

The evening before we started I had strolled round to the coach-house where Bell, who was my servant, was packing the car.

When he saw me, he glanced about him, as though to be sure that he and I were alone.

"Rowley's asked Mr Hanbury, sir, and he says we won't need any arms." He hesitated. "Is there anything else I can put in the locker below?"

There was a secret locker which few, I think, would have found. This had been made to take arms and had served its turn.

I looked at Bell.

The man was appealing to Caesar as plain as could be. Yet never before had he done this, for Hanbury and I were equal and each did as the other said.

For a moment the man's eyes held mine. Then he looked down.

"Why do you think we should take them?" said I.

"That I can't say, sir."

He was a man of few words.

"I'm glad you asked me," I said, and gave him my keys. "Mr Hanbury is perfectly right. There is no earthly reason why we should take the things, but – well, you needn't let anyone see you, but put them in."

"Very good, sir."

So was Bell also among the prophets.

We came to Salzburg quietly, entering the city at the close of a beautiful day. There we proposed to stay for a fortnight or more, and the landlord of an old-fashioned inn had been advised to expect us that very night.

We knew the house and preferred it to another hotel, for it stood in a quiet street, and so slight was its custom that a guest who was willing to pay was very well used. The kitchen was at his service, and such food as he wished was made ready at any hour: his rooms were kept as pleasant as they could be: all his ways were studied, and, indeed, so much was made of him that the host might have been his steward and the inn his private house.

There, then, we took up our quarters without any fuss, not at all sorry to be again in Salzburg and much looking forward to roving the familiar landscape, fishing the streams we remembered and drinking our fill of a sunlight that did our hearts good.

As we proposed, so did we for nearly a month, for the weather was continually fine, and I never remember keeping so healthy a holiday. Often enough we were abroad at daybreak and would take our rest by some brook in the heat of the day, and more than once we spent the night in the open, to wake up among the mountains like giants refreshed.

We did not neglect our German, but spoke with peasants and others whenever we had the chance, and we solemnly read the papers and more than once went to the play. George was far better than I, who was very halting and had to rehearse whatever I wanted to say; but at least I could understand the speech of another and, if he was content to be patient, we could converse.

We neither sought adventures nor found them and met with nothing more startling than a catch of five great trout in one afternoon. Of this we were very proud, for on no other day did we ever catch more than two, and on two out of three we caught none, for, though we enjoyed our angling, I fear the show we made was beneath contempt.

Bell or Rowley went always with us, and often we took the two, for they were both countrymen and were never, I think, so happy as when they were among meadows and within sound of a stream.

So we lived and moved very simply, till the twenty-eighth day of June.

That day we left Salzburg betimes, with both the servants and a hamper of food and drink. We drove deep into Carinthia, intending to prove once more that gracious water which had yielded our famous catch and more than half expecting to pass the night that followed under the stars.

For the first time the weather was sultry, which seemed to predict a storm, but the heaven was clear enough, and, when about sundown George Hanbury caught and landed two very fine trout, we determined to stay thereabouts and to fish the same stream the next day. Whilst we were busy, Bell and Rowley had found a little clearing in the heart of a wood and, since this was very private and was fed by a track by which we could bring up the car, we were very soon eating our supper within its green walls.

There had been no cool of the day, and when the meal was over, Hanbury and I went strolling to take the air. Of this there was very little and I was just wondering whether we should not have been wiser to rest on the brow of some hill, when, happening to look skywards, I perceived that half the heaven was blotted out.

That the storm we had feared was coming was now very plain, and, since we were not at all ready to defy a downpour, we decided to run for Salzburg without delay.

Ten minutes later we had taken the road, and, though I had hoped that we might run out of the storm, before we had covered ten miles the lightning began to play.

I never remember such a night.

The elements might have agreed to dispute our passage. Thunder and lightning apart – and these were monstrous – the tempest beset us as the seas a labouring ship; so savage was the rage of the wind that I expected every moment our hood to be carried away, while the violence and volume of the rain beggar description.

Our progress being so hampered, it soon became plain that, unless the storm abated, our journey to Salzburg would take twice as long as it should, and, after a little discussion, we decided to make for St Martin, which was a village we knew. This lay some forty miles off, and, though we might have found shelter nearer to hand, the landlord of the inn at St Martin was our very good friend and would, we knew, make us welcome, though we came as thieves in the night.

Now, had it been day, so well did we know the country that, rain or shine, we should have been at St Martin within the hour, but, with none of our landmarks to guide us and the lightning, the rain and the darkness confounding our sight, we had to depend upon signposts until we should strike some road which could not be disguised. And this was the devil; for, though we had a searchlight with which to illumine the legends the signposts bore, so dense was the rain that they could not be read from the car, and Bell and Rowley, who took it in turns to alight, were very soon drenched to the skin.

At last we came to cross roads that seemed familiar, but, though George Hanbury would have chanced it, I turned the beam on to the signpost and Rowley got out.

He had not been gone ten seconds when I heard a deep voice speaking German at the door he had used.

"Your Highness will please to enter."

Another younger man answered.

"I demand to be told where I'm going. I demand – "

The first speaker cut short the protest.

"Your Highness will enter the car."

There was a moment's silence.

Then –

"Oh, damn the rain," said the younger sullenly, as though, I thought, to suggest that but for the foulness of the weather he would have refused to comply.

With that, he entered the Rolls and flung himself down beside Bell. His companion followed heavily.

It was, of course, plain that the elder, if not both of the strangers had been expecting some car and that, when we stopped at the place and time appointed, he had directly assumed that ours was the car that he sought. On such a night such a mistake was natural, and, since all the light in the Rolls was the hooded glow that illumined the instrument board, I was not at all surprised that even his entry had not discovered his mistake.

Hanbury's lips were close to my ear.

"Dirty work," he whispered. "Let's carry them on to St Martin and see what's what."

As a figure whipped under the curtain I let in the clutch.

"We're all right, sir," said Rowley. "The road's straight ahead."

"Good," said Hanbury. "Shut the door behind you, but don't sit down."

There was a moment's silence, broken by the slam of the door.

Then –

"What the devil's this?" cried the man who had spoken first.

The question was put in German, and Hanbury answered at once.

"That's what I was going to ask you."

"Who are you? And what is this car?"

"It happens to be mine," said Hanbury.

The younger man let out a yell.

"My name's Duke – "

"*Silence!*" roared the other, rising. "Tell your chauffeur to – "

Whatever else was said was not to be heard, for the Duke was shouting like a madman and trying his best to make the other give way, the wind was slamming at the canvas as though it would drive it in and a long peal of thunder diminished all lesser noise.

Hanbury was speaking.

"Your Highness may rest assured that we are not going to stop."

"I tell you," raged the other...

"Understand this," said Hanbury. "I take no orders from you."

For a moment there was no sound behind me but the heavy, rapid breathing of a furious man at bay. The next instant all was uproar.

Though I could see nothing, I guessed that the man had drawn arms. And so it was.

Exactly what followed I do not think anyone can tell, for, seeing no reason to stop, I continued to drive the car at a good round pace, and this confounded the confusion which the darkness and confinement made. Bell was involved with the Duke, who had been thrown upon him, and could not get free; Rowley and the other were grappled and were swaying and stumbling and striking their heads on the hood: George had the fellow by the wrist and was being flung to and fro in his efforts to point the weapon out of harm's way, and everyone, I think, was raving to try to make himself heard. In the midst of all this disorder the pistol was fired, and the ear-splitting shock of the explosion brought us all, more or less, to our knees. Without so much as thinking, I set a foot on the brake, and when we had come to a standstill, I found the struggle over and George and the servants behind me regarding their late opponent, who was back on the seat.

For a moment nobody moved. Then George's hand came over and slid a heavy pistol into my lap.

"All clear," he said quietly.

I let in the clutch…

Thanks to George Hanbury's efforts, the shot had passed through the hood. Indeed, but for his energy, the battle must have gone to the stranger, or some one of us must have been hit; for the fellow was left-handed, and Rowley, who was on his right side, could not have captured his arm.

Here let me say that I shall not set down his true name or, indeed, the true names of some others of whom I shall tell. These and the names of some places I have been careful to change, for, if I had not done so, I could not have written so freely and more than one passage must have been excised from this tale.

As we ran into St Martin, George spoke again.

"We are coming to an inn," he said, "where my friend and I are well known. They're simple, honest people who value their friends, and, if I were to tell them that you had drawn upon us, you'd find a very rough house. I do not propose to tell them, and I'm sure you will give me no cause to change my mind."

A low laugh came from the Duke, and his fellow let out a curse.

"What the devil's your game?" he snarled.

"Frankly," said George, "it's to put you where you belong. We obviously can't do it until we know where that is, and, as this car's almost as unpleasant to argue in as to fight in, we're going to have things out in front of a fire."

The other said nothing, but I heard him suck in his breath.

"I'm Duke Paul," said the Duke suddenly. "Duke Paul of Riechtenburg; and this man's Major Grieg of the Black Hussars. He asks your game, but I'd damned well like to know his."

"We'll ask him in a minute," said Hanbury, and, with that, he said we were English and gave our names.

"I like London," said the Duke irrelevantly. "Do you remember —?" He named a revue. "I saw it thirty-three times. There was a girl in the chorus called Ruby Judge… Stung me to glory, of course, but she – she had her points. Little devil in a temper, she was. I gave her some sables one day, and because she'd wanted broadtail she shoved the lot in the fire."

There was an electric silence.

Then Grieg laughed, as though in triumph, and the blood came into my face. Though his conduct, I think, was warranting what we had done, I had an uneasy feeling that we had 'backed the wrong horse'.

Not until candles had been lighted in a great bedchamber and the four of us were gathered about a fire of logs were George

9

and I fairly able to appraise our two guests, for they were in uniform, and the deep collars of their greatcoats had shrouded the face.

No man, I think, would have liked the look of them.

Duke Paul was a loose-lipped youth of about my age – that is to say twenty-five. His sleek hair was sandy, and his complexion most pale. Weak, idle, dissolute – as such he impressed me. There was nothing noble about him, but much that was mean, and while his manner was haughty, this arrogance was plainly at the mercy of anyone that was minded to meet his gaze. His nails were bitten to the quick.

Grieg was a man of forty, tough and thickset. His hair and his eyes were black, a perpetual frown fretted his heavy brows, and his jaw was curiously square. He was smart and well groomed and looked a soldier, accustomed to command and to obey. Neither wise nor stolid, his expression was especially grim, and I remember feeling glad that I was not his subordinate.

Both were dressed in dark blue and wore neither belts nor spurs, but, while the major's were plain, the Duke's collar and cuffs were laced with gold.

Very few words had been exchanged, and I was still wondering how best to discharge the duty which we had so impetuously shouldered, when, to my great surprise, Grieg set a chair for the Duke and then turned to Hanbury and me.

"I've been thinking things over," he said; "and if I'd been in your position I should have done the same. I – I must apologize."

Before either of us could answer –

"And what about me?" said the Duke, with his back to the fire.

The other lowered his head.

"I am at your Highness' disposal. Your Highness will deal with me on our return."

"By God, I will," said the Duke.

10

"One thing I beg, and that is that your Highness will not judge me until my case has been heard."

"Case?" cried the Duke. "Case? D'you think I don't know – "

"I beg you, sir, not to be hasty. I am, of course, under arrest, but your Highness is unattended, and if you will allow me to attend you, I will not abuse the privilege."

Here a knock fell upon the door, and Grieg was there in an instant to see what it meant.

I think a child would have seen that submission so sudden and abject was far too good to be true, but, though the Duke looked puzzled and followed his 'prisoner' with a malevolent gaze, the entrance of Bell with some liquor distracted his thoughts. The liquor including mulled wine, he let out a whoop of delight and, though I fully expected that once this diversion was over he would return to the charge, he did not do so and, beyond ignoring Grieg's presence, seemed to have shelved his displeasure and the matter from which this sprang.

To me it was plain that his silence was exactly what Grieg had desired, but, though the latter had managed to shut the Duke's mouth and was already discussing something ponderously the fury of the storm, I could not help feeling that he had other fences to fly before we parted, and that if he surmounted them all, he would be surprisingly adroit. Indeed, the end came rather sooner than I had expected, for the Duke drank more mulled wine than he could conveniently carry and was quarrelsome in his cups.

Grieg had ventured to suggest that he should retire for the night.

The Duke glared at him.

"Retire?" He spouted an oath. "Where are my clothes?"

"If your Highness could dispense for once – "

"What about a bath in the morning? Where are my sponges? Who's to shave me? What have I got to put on?"

"No one regrets more than I – "

" 'Regret', you blackguard? The only thing you regret is that you've lost your match. But for these fellows here – Where were you taking me, Grieg? Answer me that. I'd have had my things there – I don't think. And you have the nerve – "

"I implore your Highness to wait. I beg – "

"You can — well beg," raved the Duke. "You came to me this evening and said the Prince wanted me at once. You – "

"I implore your – "

"*Silence!*" roared the Duke.

Then he turned to Hanbury and me.

"Prince Nicholas of Riechtenburg is my great-uncle, and, as my father's renounced, I'm the heir to the throne. My father's cousin don't like this – the Duke Johann. He's had one or two shots at putting me out of the way, and now that the old man's failing I suppose he's quickening up. But he," – he pointed to Grieg – "he's on my great-uncle's staff. I know Johann's little crowd, and I don't drink with them, but I never dreamed that he'd got at the Prince's ADC's."

Grieg had been standing still, with his hands behind him and his eyes on the speaker's face. Now he shrugged his shoulders and turned to a chair.

As he sat leisurely down –

"Nothing so slippery," he said coolly, "as the steps of a throne."

I have never seen a mask so bluntly discarded, and I was not surprised when the Duke started forward with an oath and a burst of abuse.

The other stifled a yawn.

"Like father, like son," he said shortly. "But he had the sense to renounce."

As the Duke began to stammer with passion, I stepped to the bell. With my hand on the old bell-rope I looked at Grieg.

"I'm not concerned with your politics," said I, "but you happen to have made me your host."

"That's one way of putting it," said Grieg.

"It's my way of putting it," said I. "And as I don't like your behaviour, I suggest that you go to bed."

The man looked me up and down.

"And if I refuse," he said, rising.

"I shall order my servants to put you out of this room."

As I pulled the rope, the Duke swayed forward drunkenly, tumbler in hand.

"Wait a minute," he said. "I haven't d-done with him yet. 'Done'? I haven't begun. I – " He rocked on his feet. "And who are you to give orders? Just because – "

Bell entered the chamber.

"Show this gentleman to his room," said I.

"Very good, sir," said Bell.

He picked up Grieg's hat and coat and stood with his hand on the door.

"D-damn it," cried the Duke. "I told you I hadn't d-done with the swine. Hadn't begun. He's a traitor – an insolent traitor. And I'm going to put him in his place. Tell 'm to shut t'door."

Grieg threw back his head and laughed.

"I congratulate you," he said, "upon your – *salvage.*"

Then he turned on his heel and walked out of the room.

What happened in the next half hour may as well be imagined as set down. One drunken man is as good or as bad as another, and by the time the Duke was asleep both George and I were bitterly cursing the folly which had led us to take up his cause. Having gone so far, however, we felt that we could not leave him to the mercies of Grieg, and that at a village of which he knew less than its name. We, therefore, decided that next morning we must in decency carry him where he wished and that, after that, we would wash our hands of a business which could breed nothing but trouble and was thankless indeed.

We then spun a coin to determine which of us two should pass the night in the chamber in which the Duke slept, and when – I confess, to my relief – the lot had fallen upon George, I bade him 'Good night' and was glad to get out of the room.

Rowley met me at the foot of the staircase to say that Bell was watching the major's door, but I thought this precaution needless and bade them take their rest by the side of the car. This was happily simple, for, since there was no coach-house but a gigantic hall, I had driven the car clean into the inn itself, to the great content of the landlord and all his staff, who were never tired of regarding so unfamiliar a guest.

I also told the servants that if Grieg sought to leave the house they were to let him go, for I had no wish at all to hold him prisoner or, indeed, to set eyes on him again. With that, I gave Bell the pistol which George had taken from Grieg, in case the latter should endeavour to damage the car. Such an attempt seemed to me likely enough, for, since his abduction of the Duke had so miscarried, it would plainly be to his interest to apprise those he served of his failure *before the Duke reappeared*: and, as he could scarcely expect assistance from us, to delay the Duke's return was the best he could do.

Bell took the pistol, and then with an air of apology offered me one in its stead.

"I should go armed, sir," he said, "until we're out of the wood."

I slid the thing into my pocket and went to my bed.

Nothing disturbed me that night, and I was afoot at seven of a beautiful day.

We had brought a suitcase from Salzburg, and the landlord remembered our ways, so Bell had made everything ready for me to bathe and change. As soon as my toilet was done I went straight to Hanbury's room, to find him smoking at the window and the Duke still sleeping like the dead. While George was dressing I took his place in the room, and then between us we persuaded the Duke to rise.

The latter refused point-blank to leave his bed, upbraiding us fiercely for rousing him and declaring that the pain in his head was not to be borne. On our persisting, he started to curse and swear and threw a glass at Hanbury when at last he ripped off the clothes. Once he was up, however, he took himself in hand and behaved more civilly, though he gave us no thanks.

Breakfast he would not, but demanded some China tea. When I told him that no sort of tea was to be had of such an inn, he abused the house with great freedom and asked me what the devil I meant by bringing a man of his standing to such a place. At that, I called Bell and told him to bring some spring water, commending this to the Duke as likely to serve his distemper rather better than anything else, and, though he looked very black and muttered a rudeness which I think he had not the courage to say aloud, I am glad to remember that he presently took my advice.

Then he looked out of the window and saw the Rolls.

"That's more like it," he said. "When do we start?"

"As soon as you're ready," said I, "we'll drive you wherever you please."

"I must get back to Vigil," said he. "We must be miles over the border, but once we're in Riechtenburg, it'll take us no more than an hour."

"That's right," said Hanbury, tracing the way on the map. "West and by North from here, and a three hours' run. Vigil's the chief town, of course."

"Complete with palace," said the Duke. "The Prince is there now. By rights he should be in the country, but he's been too ill to be moved. I'll go there straight," he continued, "and put him wise. This scoundrel Grieg must be – By the way, where is Grieg?"

"He hasn't appeared," said I.

"So much the better," said the Duke. "Are you ready to go?"

"The point is this," said Hanbury. "We're sick of the sight of the fellow, but we're not prepared to hang him round the innkeeper's neck."

"Why not?" said the Duke.

"It's not fair to the innkeeper," said George. "He's a very decent fellow, and Grieg'll raise all hell when he finds we're gone."

"Damn it," cried the other, "what does that matter to me? If – "

Here Bell entered the room, salver in hand.

"The major has gone, sir," he reported. "By way of the window, I think. His bed was untouched, and I found this note on the floor."

A twisted sheet of paper was superscribed *Duke Paul*.

The message within was printed rudely enough.

There is now no harm in your knowing that your great-uncle Prince Nicholas VII died yesterday evening at a quarter to six. At nine o'clock this morning Prince Johann will be proclaimed.

The Duke turned very pale, and a hand went up to his mouth. George and I glanced at each other.

As we did so, the clock of the village church beat out the hour. Nine o'clock.

2

A Lady of High Degree

Half an hour had gone by, and we were again upon the road.

We were not bound for Vigil or even for Riechtenburg, but for a castle in Carinthia which lay to the east of St Martin, some seventy miles away. This was the seat of the Riechtenburg second line, now alone represented, it seemed, by the Grand Duchess Leonie, to whom the Duke was betrothed.

So much our guest had vouchsafed us, after a deplorable scene, in which he breathed enough threatenings to fill up a book, swore that the army was faithful and would follow him to the death and instanced a score of times the love, esteem and veneration in which he was held by the people that he vas to rule. In view of all these protests, we counselled his immediate departure, promising to have him at Vigil before it was noon; but he steadfastly ignored our entreaties to enter the car until he conceived the idea of himself acquainting his fiancée with what was afoot. Then he would wait for nothing, raving like any madman because we must look at the map, but I fear that, had her castle stood in Riechtenburg instead of in the opposite direction to that principality, he would not have been so instant that we should proceed.

In a word, the man was 'rattled.' It is not for me to blame him, for what I should have done in his case I do not know; but

I cannot pretend that he cut a princely figure, and I could not help wondering whether his cousin Johann, usurper or no, would not rule his people at least as well.

To be perfectly frank, both George and I were glad to be quit of the duty of visiting Riechtenburg. Had Duke Paul been other than he was, if his presence had inspired any feelings but those of scorn and dislike, we should both have been happy to help him to try to save the game; but the prospect of escorting to Vigil so objectionable a youth, there perhaps to meet with a reception which, however unpleasant, we could not honestly condemn was, I think, not unnaturally, one which we were thankful to forego. Indeed, we looked forward cheerfully to our approaching release, and that with a clear conscience, for if we had had our way, we should have been driving for Vigil as hard as we could.

Now, well as we knew Carinthia, we had never passed by Anger, the Grand Duchess Leonie's home, and I cannot forget the impression of vanished splendour which my first sight of it evoked.

To reach it, we left the valleys and climbed by the side of a torrent into the hills. Our road, though shown upon the map, was for the last three miles as good as private, for so far as I saw, it served no other dwelling, but led directly to the castle and there came to an end. This was by no means unusual, for the great houses of those parts are nearly always retired, and, since the estates about them are seldom if ever fenced, one who is touring at random can never tell what some lane or by-road may bring forth.

Our way was girt thick with timber, and, since the trees were in leaf, I at the wheel could see nothing except that we had entered a gorge and were climbing between two shoulders that towered on either side. At length, as we rounded a beechwood, the sides of the gorge fell away, or rather the gorge itself bellied into an ample circus, once, no doubt, all forest, but now greensward. This was the head of the gorge, for the mountains stood round in a ring, and on the far side of the circus a great cascade fell down in a single leap. At its base the waters parted and ran to right and to left, meeting again in the midst of the great greensward to form the angry torrent by the side of which we had come. And on the island, so made, rose the castle itself – a grey, lichened pile, with the water fretting its sides and the trees stretching out great boughs to overhang its battlements and chafe its towers. The ramparts had been made into a terrace, perhaps a century ago, and seven great windows argued a lofty gallery upon the south. These were shuttered within, and nearly every one was short of a pane. Between each window stood a statue, plainly of bronze, bearing aloft a lantern which must have been three feet high. There had no doubt been a drawbridge, but this was gone: in its room four leopards held up a bridge of stone. In niches above the gateway stood two bronze men-at-arms, between whom hung a great bell. Above this their hands were raised as though to strike, and I afterwards found that their arms were controlled by pulleys and that years ago they had served the castle clock. Now a clapper had been put to the bell, and the rope which dangled from this was hitched to one side of the archway, for those who came to pull. Porter there was none, and, but for some cows in the meadow and a little child to tend them, there was no sign of life.

When I came to the bridge, I slowed down.

"Go on. Drive in," said the Duke. "And sound the horn."

More to please myself than my guest, I did his bidding, for I had a mind to see the courtyard within; but I sounded the bulb horn gently, for the other would have cried 'Havoc!' in such a place.

As I passed under the archway, the Duke exclaimed with impatience and, leaning across me, sounded the electric horn.

In that gesture you have the man.

Arrogant, mannerless, strong to commit an offence which those it offended would lay to another's charge – for it was I that was driving and I that had the horn-button under my hand…

The noise, of course, was monstrous. The old walls bandied it frantically, and the cliffs beyond gave it back: a muster of terrified pigeons took clumsy flight: two dogs were barking like mad things, and I sat still fuming and waiting for the echoes to die.

As the Duke descended, a woman's clear voice rang out.

"To what do I owe this pleasure?"

The words came from behind me. I did not turn, but looked into the driving mirror to see a girl sitting square on a great bay horse.

She had followed us under the archway and was now framed by its mouth. I could see that her hair was dark and her colour high. She sat astride and was wearing riding-trousers that fitted her very well: her rough straw hat was bound with a bright red kerchief, and her white silk shirt lay open about her throat.

As the Duke approached, she drew off her right-hand glove and, when he uncovered, she leaned down ever so slightly and put her bare hand into his. I saw him kiss her fingers and look up into her face.

"Leonie," he said, "they've done it on me. The old man died last evening, and Johann was proclaimed this morning at nine o'clock."

The Grand Duchess never moved.

"Why are you here?" she said.

"Grieg came for me yesterday evening. The Prince wanted me, he said. He had a blind car, and before I knew where I was we were out of the city and flicking hell for leather along the Austrian road. I'd have broken his neck, but he shoved a gun in my ribs. About half past ten we got out on some country road. I've never seen such rain. Then another car comes up and Grieg tells me to get inside. You couldn't argue the point in rain like that. I tell you it was too awful. Besides, he had a gun…

"Well, it was the wrong car. Belonged to these English fellows – they'd been catching fish. I put them wise, and between us we flattened Grieg out. Spent the night at some village in a flyblown inn. Grieg cleared out in the night and left this note." I saw a paper pass. "I was just leaving for Vigil when somebody brought it in."

The Grand Duchess read the note and handed it back. Then she spoke in English as clear and clean as could be.

"Why are you here?"

The Duke took out cigarettes.

"To put you wise, of course, Leonie."

"You could have telephoned: and – well, unless you mean to sit down under – "

"Of course I don't," cried the Duke.

"Then why aren't you at Vigil?"

"I'm going," said the Duke. "I'm going." He lighted a cigarette and stared at its fiery end. "So you advise – "

The Grand Duchess laughed.

"Nothing, Paul. I'm not – interested."

The Duke looked up sharply.

"I should have thought," he began.

"I know. Most people would."

"Don't you want to be Princess?"

"I never did," said the girl: "but I used to have a weakness for seeing people come by their rights. But you've got me out of that."

I cannot describe the scorn with which her words were spoken. It was a quiet, cold disdain, more evident to us, I fancy, than to the Duke himself. This and her use of English made me feel sure that she was determined that we strangers should know the truth, lest we should hold her shameless in being betrothed to such a man.

"Hang it, Leonie," said the Duke. "I didn't come for a pi-jaw."

"I know. You came for advice. Or was it to put me wise? Never mind. I've no advice to give you, but I can give you some news."

"News?"

21

"News. That note's a lie. It was very nearly true. Grieg, of course, hoped it was true, and he guessed that, true or false, it would keep you out of Vigil for several hours. *The Prince had a stroke last night at half past five. Everyone thought it was the end, but at half past six he rallied and at eight o'clock this morning he was doing extremely well.*"

"You're joking," cried the Duke hoarsely.

"Of course I'm not," said the girl. "Marya Dresden telephoned to me last night. And she rang up again this morning to tell me I needn't come."

The Duke whooped, flung his hat into the air and began to dance grotesquely and to play a phantom banjo…

That the man would now expect us to drive him to Vigil forthwith I had no doubt, and, all things considered, I did not see how we could well refuse to convey him at least as far as the frontier of Riechtenburg. I, therefore, started the engine and set about turning the car.

There was not too much room, for an idle fountain stood in the middle of the court, and, the outlet of this being in course of repair, the court itself had been opened, to let a man come at the drain.

By the time, therefore, that I had gone about, the Grand Duchess was off her horse, which a groom was leading away, and the Duke was urging some point with a sheepish look on his face.

As I brought the car to rest, the Grand Duchess cut him short.

"I've told you," she said, using German, "I do not care. I wish you no ill, of course. But I wouldn't lift a finger to save your throne."

With that, she turned her head and her eyes met mine.

I was gazing at her as at something which is not of this world; for, now that I saw her clearly, her beauty was so excelling that, for all the good they did me, I might have had no manners and indeed no one of the senses, save only that of sight.

She had pulled off her hat, and her soft, short hair was so black that the lights in its waves were blue. Her nose was aquiline, and her steady, grave eyes were grey. Her mouth was especially lovely, but very proud: her colour was high and healthy and her skin very white and, indeed, her whole countenance was fine and fresh and vivid as a flower may be in a garden before the sun is high. She was slim and tall for a woman and stood very well. There was nothing about her which was not feminine, yet it was very plain that her little finger was thicker than the Duke's loins. Her look was keen and fearless, her temples were wise, and I have never seen such dignity so artlessly displayed.

As I gazed, I saw her displeasure and hastily bowed my head to examine the instrument-board, but my cheeks and my ears were burning, and so, when I think of that moment, they do to this day.

The Grand Duchess was speaking in English.

"You may as well introduce them if I am to give them lunch."

The words stung like a whip, and almost before I knew it I was standing by the side of the car with my hat in my hand.

I addressed myself to the Duke.

"We never lunch," I said quietly, "but, if you'd like us to give you a lift to Vigil, we'll throw a fly over that water and be back here in two hours."

The Duke stared at me.

"D'you mean you never – "

"Never," said I shortly, and glanced at my watch. "Shall we say half past one?"

"That'll suit me all right," said the Duke. "But don't you want a drink, or – "

But I was back in my seat.

"At half past one," I said, smiling, and let in the clutch.

Now George, who had never descended, was up on his feet, and the servants had only just time to get aboard: when, therefore, the car shot forward, each clawed hold of the other and all fell down in a heap upon the back seat, presenting a spectacle which must have been more diverting than the antics of any clowns. But the first I knew of it was the long, fresh peal of a girl's laughter ringing under the archway as the Rolls passed over the bridge.

We did not fish, but, since on leaving Salzburg we had taken food for two days, we lunched in a blowing meadow ten miles away.

I cannot pretend that we made a festive meal.

We had put ourselves out and about for a notorious wastrel, who accepted our services as though the privilege of doing them greatly outweighed their worth: I had forgotten my manners in a most unfortunate way, and in return we had been deliberately insulted by a girl who was plainly no more than twenty years old, who, by her relation to the Duke, might very well be considered to be in our debt: my zeal to be gone had made us a laughing-stock – a point upon which the Grand Duchess had taken care to insist; and, worst of all, I had in my haste engaged us to suffer for another five hours a well-nigh insufferable guest.

However, there was nothing to be done, and I gratefully remember that George very handsomely declined to blame me at all, declaring that if there had been anything to retrieve, I had much more than retrieved it by my very pointed refusal to meet the Grand Duchess at all, "while as for staring," he added, "I don't know what the hussy expects. If she likes to look like a Madonna, talk like Queen Elizabeth and get her clothes made in Savile Row, anyone may be pardoned for staring. And now let's go back and swallow the rest of our gruel. I'm going to drive and you're going to sit with me, and if the Duke don't like the back seat he can damned well sit on the floor."

At the hour appointed we were back in the old courtyard.

A manservant saw our coming and disappeared, but, as though to prove our patience, nobody came to the door; and after waiting ten minutes I bade Rowley ring the bell.

After another five minutes the manservant reappeared and descended the steps. I saw that the man was English.

"Her Highness hopes, sir," he said, "that you will come in."

"Beg her Highness to excuse us," I said. "And tell his Highness Duke Paul that, if he has no objection, we are anxious to start at once."

"Very good, sir," said the man, and withdrew.

For a moment or two we sat waiting. Then the Grand Duchess appeared at the head of the steps.

"So I must come myself," she said quietly.

Hanbury and I uncovered, but sat where we were.

"I'm sorry I spoke so rudely and I should like to be friends."

I opened my door and alighted, and Hanbury followed me out.

"The fault was mine," I stammered, with my eyes on the ground.

As though I had not spoken she turned to George.

"I saw you looking at the bay. If you're interested in horses, I can show you a better than he."

"We'd love to see him," said Hanbury.

She led the way over the cobbles and under another arch…

She never addressed me once, but when we had seen her three hunters she led us into the house by another way. I hardly looked at her, except when her back was turned, but she had changed her clothes for a dress of an old rose colour which suited her very well.

As we came into a hall, a woman of many summers rose from a table at which she was writing a note, and the Duke cried 'Hullo' from the sofa on which he sprawled.

The Grand Duchess introduced us, and I was astonished to find that the Duke, who must have informed her, had so well remembered our names.

"My great-aunt, Mrs Scarlett," she said. And then, "My mother was English. That's why I speak so well."

"We needn't start yet," said the Duke. "Sit down and have a brandy. I've tasted worse."

Before we could make any answer, a telephone-bell was ringing somewhere at hand,

The Grand Duchess flashed to a corner, and I heard her reply.

"Yes…this is Anger. Yes, Marya, this is me… He's here, he's here, Marya. He's just going to start for Vigil: he ought to be there by six… He'll tell you himself: I can't tell you over the line, but… What?… I can't quite hear, Marya. 'Tell him…' " She took the second earpiece and listened with all her might. "Yes, I've got that. I will. And… Very well. At eight o'clock this evening, if you've no news before. Goodbye, Marya."

She put the receiver back and turned to the Duke.

"The Prince is worse," she said. "The doctors won't say he's sinking, but he's awfully bad. Marya says you must come as quick as ever you can. Her words were 'Tell him it's vital – you can guess what I mean.' "

The Duke was biting his nails.

"It's all damned fine," he said. "These sort of shows can't be rushed. What on earth did you say I was here for?"

The Grand Duchess stared at him.

"Why shouldn't I say so? What do you propose to do?"

"Go carefully," said the Duke. "I'm not at all sure that it's wise to go bursting back."

"I suppose by 'wise' you mean 'safe'?"

Mrs Scarlett covered her eyes, but the Duke's withers were unwrung.

"It's all Weber's fault," he cried, "for withdrawing those blasted police. They police me in Paris and London. Why the devil don't they police me at home?" He got to his feet. "I'll ring him up and tell him to send some along."

The Grand Duchess appeared to hesitate. Then she went to his side.

26

"Paul," she said, "listen to me. It's vital that you should get back and state your case. Till you appear and start talking, Johann, Grieg and Co. can have it all their own way: but once the Prince knows what's happened, Johann won't dare to touch you – that's common sense. And now get ready. *I'm coming with you.*" The Duke started, and the old lady rose to her feet. "I may as well be at Vigil, and – well, it'd rather amuse me to flatten Johann."

Before he could answer she was gone, and, since there was no point in our waiting, we took our leave of her great-aunt and made our way back to the car.

I was astounded at this complete change of front. Her declarations apart, three hours ago I could have sworn that the girl did not care a farthing whether Duke Paul or his cousin came to the throne. More. She had seemed to care for his honour less than he cared for it himself. This in cold blood. Such an outlook had not surprised me. To know him was to lose interest in such a man. And now…

As Hanbury took his seat, I reflected that it was at least more pleasant to carry to Vigil one who was worth her salt.

We were twenty miles from the frontier when I saw a closed car ahead by the side of the road. Of this I thought little enough, but we had encountered very little traffic, and I think that when you are moving on empty roads you always observe a car which is standing still.

As we drew near, I could see that someone was standing beside the car and was watching us closely, as though he were more than half minded to signal to us to stop; but, when we drew nearer, I saw him turn back to his car and shake his head.

I was wondering what was his business and for whom, if not us, he was watching, when he looked round again. The next instant he was out in the road and was waving his arms.

Hanbury spoke over his shoulder.

"Am I to stop?"

"What? Yes. Stop!" cried the Duke. "Stop, man, stop! *It's the police.* Good old Weber." I heard him slap his thigh. "Marya Dresden must have told him. Oh, my aunt, what a scream!"

I give his own words, as he spoke them, for, though as a rule, he spoke German, he very often used English and spoke it extremely well. But I cannot represent his jubilant tone or the awkwardness of the silence which succeeded his speech. The man was above shame.

As George set his foot upon the brake, another man came running to join the first. Both wore a grey uniform which was bound with green.

As the car stopped, they saluted.

"Pardon, your Highness," said the first, who had stripes on his sleeve, "but we have been sent to escort you."

"That's the style," said the Duke, and, without asking Hanbury or me, he bade them mount the Rolls and stand on her running-boards.

The sergeant looked ill-at-ease.

"Your Highness will excuse me," he said, "but we were instructed that your Highness would use the police car."

The Duke frowned.

The Rolls was very good-looking and moved like a bird on the wing: the other was closed and shabby and the noisy fuss of its engine promised a less pleasant ride.

"No," he said shortly. "I'm going to stay where I am. Get on the step, as I tell you, and your driver can follow behind."

"Your Highness will forgive me," said the sergeant, "but we have had special instructions not to go by the bridge at Elsa, but to follow a devious route."

There was a little silence.

Then –

"Does the chauffeur know the way?" said the Duke.

"Yes, your Highness, he does. And he alone. So – "

"Then we'll follow him," said the Duke, lighting a cigarette.

There was nothing more to be said, and, though George and I were raging inwardly, for the sake of the Grand Duchess we held our peace.

One minute later we were again under way.

Our speed was now much lower, for our pilot was not a swift car and was troubled by every rise. Very soon, moreover, it left the main road, leading us into country through which no car could hasten, for the roads were none too wide and very crooked, the hills severe and most of the turnings blind.

We had gone, I suppose, some three miles and had just descended the very deuce of a hill, when we rounded a sudden bend to see the police car at rest in the midst of the way. Where it stood, the road was sunk in a little swell of the forest which lay hereabouts, and we could not draw alongside to see what the matter might be.

As George brought the Rolls to a standstill, the sergeant stepped into the road and opened the hinder door.

"Your Highness will descend immediately."

We all stared at him.

"And no one else will move," said a voice on my left.

Instinctively we all looked round.

The other policeman was still on the running-board, half sitting on the near spare wheel, with one hand grasping the windscreen and the other a Service revolver of which he seemed none too sure.

"God in heaven," said the Duke weakly. "And I thought you were police."

The first speaker bowed.

"We flatter ourselves," he said, "a very natural mistake."

As the Duke rose, the man on my left incautiously lowered his weapon, and I hit him full in the stomach with all my might. It was, of course, a foul blow, and he crumpled and then fell sideways without a sound.

The rest was easy.

Rowley had closed with the sergeant before he could draw, and, when I descended, my man had dropped his revolver and was writhing in pain.

"Tie them up," said I, and ran for the other car.

This began to move forward when I was but six feet away, and, though I made a great effort, before I could manage to board it, I was outrun.

At once George brought up the Rolls and, almost before I was in, began to give chase.

For this piece of folly both he and I were to blame, for I was as eager as he to lay all three men by the heels. Looking back, I am ashamed that we should have been so childish, for we had won our battle and cleared our way and had only to go about to be in Vigil itself in little more than an hour. Instead of this, we went pelting through country we did not know, along roads which were so narrow that, unless the other let us, we dared not pass, in the hope, I suppose, of his being checked by traffic or meeting with some misadventure which would give him into our hand. Meanwhile we had left the servants to shift for themselves and were now but two to cope with whatever befell.

Such foolishness had its reward.

A sudden jarring told us a tyre was punctured, and, before we could come to a standstill, two more had met the same fate.

This was, of course, out of reason, unless the man we were chasing had strewn something sharp in our way. So he had done. One of his barbs or snags is before me now – a four-spiked horror of steel, which, however idly you throw it, will always stand upon three spikes and thrust the fourth into the air. Such things were once used in warfare to lame the enemy's horse, and I afterwards found that in the Riechtenburg army they were field service stores.

We had two spare wheels, and, as luck would have it, a tube, so half an hour's hard labour would make the car fit for the road, but I fear we were out of temper with all the world, and, when the Duke protested that we should "get on to Vigil and let the — tyres go," I ignored the suggestion and Hanbury answered curtly that, even if it had not been ours, we should never so abuse such a car.

With that, we took off our coats and got to work, and the Duke flounced back on his seat and closed his eyes.

The Grand Duchess was down by my side.

"What can I do?" she said.

With the back of my hand I wiped the sweat from my brow. Then I took up one of the snags that had punctured our tyres.

"If you will walk back," said I, "and look for some more things like this. I don't know how many he dropped, but it's hardly likely he got us the first go off."

Before I had finished, she was gone and was searching the road.

By the time the Rolls was ready she had not returned: we, therefore, turned the car round with infinite care and started to go very slowly the way we had come.

Before we had gone half a mile, the road bent sharp to the right and then split into two, and, though George without hesitation swung to the left, I was by no means certain that that was our way. What was more to the point, it very soon became clear that, rightly or wrongly, the Grand Duchess had taken the other road, and, since she had to be found before we did anything else, we went about again and essayed the right-hand road.

Almost at once we found her, but, when George asked her if this was the way we had come, she said that, now that she had seen it, she was not sure and added that, for what it was worth, she had found no snags.

I did not know what to think, and, though George was now less certain that he had been right, we had just decided to return once more to the fork, when the Duke indicated a rill which leapt from between two rocks, as though from a mouth, and then fell into a trough which was cut from the trunk of a tree. This he declared he remembered, and, since that was very much more than anyone else could say, we considered the matter settled and drove ahead.

And that was the beginning of trouble for, when, after twenty minutes, we had proved his memory faithless and sought to return to the fork, we could by no means find it and only with every movement seemed to stray further afield.

The country was very blind and the roads rose and fell and twisted as though bewitched; there were no fingerposts to help us, and when we looked for the map it was not to be found.

After an hour of wandering, George brought the car to rest by the side of the road.

"What the hell's the matter now?" said the Duke.

George spoke over his shoulder.

"For one thing," he said, "I'm tired. I've stopped and started and turned and backed till I can't feel the clutch. Add to that that I've changed two wheels and permanently injured my brain, trying to find the way which you insisted you knew." He sighed there, and I began to shake with laughter. "Well, that's one reason. If you want another, *we've exactly half a gallon of petrol left*. We had ample to get to Vigil, but I meant to fill up at the frontier – just in case. But that was before the mix-up... I don't want to point no fingers and I'm perfectly ready to bear my share of the blame. I've been driving, and the dial's right under my nose. But it's all this mucking about that's run us dry."

There was an uneasy silence.

Then –

"How far," said the Duke, "will half a gallon get us?"

George raised his eyebrows.

"In this going, employed with care, about five miles."

With that, he turned to me and demanded a cigarette.

I had walked three miles across country and seen neither man nor beast nor any sort of building but a cottage that had been burned down, when I came to the edge of a bluff, to see, far below me, fair meadows and in their midst an abbey with its attendant farm.

The scene made as pretty a picture as ever I saw, for the sun was setting and the valley was full of red light. A stream flowed through the meadows, and cattle were slaking their thirst on their way by a ford: the water was running golden, and everything, great and little, was throwing its clean-cut shadow upon the turf. Smoke was rising from the buildings, but I saw neither monks nor nuns, and the view of a ruinous cloister suggested that the place was no longer a covert of Holy Church. Still it was a decent homestead, at which, if need be, the Grand Duchess could pass the night: and that was what I was seeking, for, unless we could come by some petrol, we could not go on and, before we set our face to the frontier, the servants had to be found.

A road ran out of the valley, and, so far as I was able, I marked the line that it took. Then I returned to the Rolls and made my report.

"Can they give us petrol?" said the Duke sullenly.

"We'll know when we get there," said I.

He flung himself back on his seat and held his peace.

It was an anxious journey, for dusk was upon us and I had to guess the way: but, after much disappointment, we ran down a long steep hill and into the valley I sought.

We crossed the stream by a bridge of old grey stone, and a moment later we saw the abbey ahead with the bluff on its left.

And there the engine fainted, for lack of fuel...

In spite of my walk, George was more weary than I, for his rest had been but broken the night before. I, therefore, alighted and started to walk to the farm, which lay a lady's mile distant at the end of the road.

The Grand Duchess lifted her voice.

"Where are you going?"

"For petrol," I answered. "And, if I can't have it, for horses to pull us in."

"I will go," she said shortly, stepping down into the road.

"Thank you," said I, "but it's nothing. Besides, you can't go alone."

"Then I will go with you," she said, "for the look of the thing."

We began to walk in silence towards the farm.

The Grand Duchess was speaking.

"Has Paul thanked you once for anything that you've done?"

"We don't want any thanks," said I. "And we haven't done very much."

"I thank you," she said quietly.

I did not know what to reply and so said nothing, but walked along, like a fool, with my eyes on the ground. But the words had been gently spoken, and I felt more than paid.

"If they can't give us petrol," she said, "what shall we do?"

"I shall ride to the nearest garage. Then I must find the servants, and then we'll drive to Vigil, if you're not too tired."

"This delay's unlucky," she said. "By keeping out of the picture, Paul is playing directly into his cousin's hand. You see, he should be on parade – especially now. The Prince is dying, and Paul is his rightful heir. There's no shadow of doubt about that. And everyone will support him – *provided that he himself doesn't let them down*. If he does, if he's not there at the moment for them to support, to sign proclamations and orders, to appear on the balcony – well, people are only human... If you've got a King you must play him, or the other side will."

"But if," said I, "if he's the heir apparent – "

"Paul isn't popular," she said. "It isn't his fault – he was spoiled. Plenty of people believe that he doesn't value the throne. If he takes his place and claims it, he'll have it, because it's his right. But, if he doesn't, they'll throw up their hats for Johann. And that's why we *must* get to Vigil as soon as we possibly can."

"We'll do our utmost," I said. "I promise you that."

The Grand Duchess lifted her head and spoke to the sky.

"Paul's his worst enemy," she said, "and always was. Far worse than Johann. He's lost so many games, because he couldn't be bothered to play the right cards. But he – he mustn't throw this away."

I made no answer, but stepped along by her side, very well aware of her beauty and thankful to find her so friendly and frank of speech.

Presently she spoke of England and asked of the life we led. And I told her of Maintenance and Wiltshire and how we hunted all the winter and spent more hours in the open than under a roof.

"That's right," she said gravely. "That's the way we were meant to live. Up and down with the sun and three meals a day."

I walked clean into the trap.

"One breaks it sometimes," said I, "but it's a very good rule."

"I agree," said the Grand Duchess. And then, "I – I thought you never lunched."

I could feel her eyes upon me, but, when at last I looked round, she was gazing into the distance with the faintest smile on her face.

"I – I have nothing to say," I stammered.

The Grand Duchess' smile deepened.

"No one," she said, "could accuse *you* of being changeable."

As we drew near the buildings, I could see that the abbey had been built in the form of a square; but two sides of this were gone. What I had taken for the church was the refectory: this with the ancient kitchen still made one side of the square and ran at right angles to a mansion which made the other. I say 'a mansion' for lack of a better word, but the face of it was not changed and it looked the private dwelling of someone of note. Along the refectory some twenty yards of cloister were well preserved, but, except for its bench and pavement, the rest was gone, though the mansion still bore the piers from which its arches had sprung.

No lights were burning in the house, the door of which was set wide, but two dogs came towards us, baying, and a man who was sitting by the doorway rose up and called them to heel.

I could not see him very well, for the daylight was almost gone, but he was a big, burly fellow and clearly the farmer or master of the place.

When the Grand Duchess asked for petrol, he shook his head.

"I have none," he said slowly. "I have an old car, but that is away for repairs, and all the spirit I have is in her tank. Have you far to go, madam?"

"As far as the nearest pump."

"I see. Well, that is at Bariche, on the Riechtenburg road."

"How far is Bariche?"

"A matter of fifteen miles."

My companion drew in her breath.

"We must have petrol," she said. "Can you lend us a horse?"

"Not to travel that distance, madam. My horses have done their day's work."

"It shall be stabled at Bariche, and I will deposit its value against its return."

The other shook his head.

"Tomorrow, madam," he said. "But not tonight. Where is your car?"

"This side of the bridge," said my lady. "A mile away."

"I do not see its lamps," said the other.

"Because they are not turned on."

The man appeared to hesitate.

Then –

"I will give you shelter," he said, and called for lights.

"I do not want shelter," said my lady. "I want a horse."

As a man came clumping with a lantern –

"In any event," said the farmer, "I will go with you to your car."

With that, he took the lantern and bade the man turn out a yoke of oxen and bring them down to the bridge.

"It is damp in the meadows," he said.

The Grand Duchess shrugged her shoulders and turned to me.

"*Force majeure*," she said.

"I will walk to Bariche," said I.

"And lose yourself by the way. No. There is nothing to be done. At dawn, perhaps…"

She was right. There was nothing to be done. Bell and Rowley must wait and so must the Duke. The farmer was not a peasant that could be bluffed or bribed. In his way he would help us or not at all.

"Will you wait here?" said I. "If we can do nothing till daybreak, we may as well bring in the car."

The girl hesitated. Then –

"Paul will be hasty," she said. "I think I had better come."

"I will handle him," said I. "Your shoes were not meant for these roads." I stepped to the bench from which the man had risen and felt the stone. "The stone is still warm and will be for half an hour. But we shall be here before then."

"Very well," said the Grand Duchess. "Don't let Paul play the fool."

The farmer was a man of few words. When I asked him the way to Bariche, he answered that it lay to the South: when I asked him if he could lodge us, he nodded his head; and, when I observed that his home was very handsome, he spoke to one of his dogs.

As we approached the car, I took the lead and, cheerfully hailing the others, cried out that we were in luck, for that we could have food and lodging of an excellent sort, that petrol would be brought in the morning and that oxen were coming to draw the car to the farm. My ruse, however, was a failure; for the Duke began to rave like a madman, demanding to be carried to Vigil, as though we were slaves of some lamp, now swearing that we had betrayed him and now reviling the car, talking all manner of nonsense about his position and birth and declaring that we might be glad to sleep where we could, but that such was not the habit of royalty or indeed of any person of high estate.

Hanbury was speaking wearily.

"The reasons for this display are three. The first is he wants a cocktail: the second, he's out of cigarettes: and the third, he regrets having chucked his excellent gold cigarette-case – merely because it was empty – into the stream."

Once more, remembering my promise, I strove to appease the Duke's wrath, although, I confess, I was sorely tempted to cool it by throwing him after his bauble into the stream: but, as was to be expected, I might have saved my breath, for he cut me short by announcing that he was not accustomed to having his commands disobeyed.

"Needs must," said I shortly. "We'll breakfast over the border with any luck."

The Duke peered at the farmer, who was now alongside.

"You've got petrol, of course," he blustered. "You can't deceive me. How many cans can I have at a pound apiece?"

The farmer raised his lantern, until he could see the Duke's face. For a moment he regarded him steadily. Then he lowered the light.

"The misfortune is mine," he said quietly. "I have no petrol. But I have a kitchen and a cellar of which I am not ashamed."

I was greatly relieved, for the Duke's tone was high and mighty, and I had not expected an answer one half so smooth. I, therefore, made haste to suggest that he and George and the farmer should proceed to the house, while I came on with the oxen, soon to arrive. While he was hesitating, I gave him a cigarette, and I think that settled the matter, for, when he had lit it, he spat out an oath or two and flung out of the car.

The oxen moved very slowly, and nearly an hour had gone by before I was led to a handsomely furnished parlour – which once, I should say, had been the abbot's – with arras upon its walls. The Rolls was bestowed in an outhouse of which I had taken the key, and, since her bonnet was locked, could come to no harm. And I had washed in a horse trough and was ready enough for a meal.

A table had been set in the parlour and decently laid for four, and the chamber was pleasantly lighted by lamps which hung from the roof.

The Duke was there, dozing, and Hanbury was reading a book.

"We've fallen soft," said George. "This is some cove's private house. The book-plates suggest that his name is Martin Egge. I imagine the farmer's his bailiff. I hope he's a right to lodge us, but I'm damned well not going to ask."

Be sure I agreed with him.

A good, plain dinner was served by two young girls, and the Duke said the wine would pass, but Hanbury and I drank ale.

The Grand Duchess was very silent, but thanked me for sending her dressing-case up to her room.

When the meal was over, our host came into the parlour and stood blinking in the light of the lamp.

"We have to thank you," said my lady. "You are treating us very well."

The other bowed.

"I am bailiff to Baron Veners, madam, whose house this is. He would wish me to entertain strangers who have lost their way."

"And to speed them," said the Grand Duchess, "by sending a man for petrol at break of day."

"That is understood, madam."

He bowed again and withdrew.

Very soon after, the Grand Duchess took her leave.

As I opened the door, she looked me full in the eyes.

"Who's Baron Veners?" she murmured.

The next moment she was gone.

I made my way to the window and stood looking out into the night.

There was much that was strange about the bailiff and unusual about the place. The name on the book-plates was not Veners. The house was at our disposal, and food and wine, but not a horse to help us to go our ways. But I was tired and had had my fill of riddles, and I think there comes a time when the evil of the day is sufficient and a man will swallow his fortune without asking whence it came. The Grand Duchess, however, was not the one to ask an idle question or to set a tired man thinking for nothing at all.

Wearily enough, I started to marshal my wits...

As I did so, without and below the window somebody coughed.

I leaned out to see the bailiff, sitting as we had found him, on the bench by the door. This was open, and his shape was outlined against the blur of light which was shed by a lamp in the hall. His great head was up, and he was smoking placidly, with his heavy arms folded and his eyes on the West.

I drew in my head and strove to appraise the man.

He had not been uncivil, yet he had not been polite: he had been firm, but not downright: his air was not that of a soldier, nor that of a rogue, but of something betwixt and between – I could not think what. I did not distrust the fellow, but I had the feeling that, though he had given us shelter, he had done so neither for our sake nor yet for his own. He had seemed, I recalled, to doubt the presence of the car and had plainly decided to go and see for himself. He had called for a lantern, although night had not fallen and only a blind man could ever have missed the way. When I would have talked, he would not: and, when the Duke had crossed him, he passed it by. These things were consistent with his manner – the wilful, deliberate manner of a masterful man whose eyes are upon his duty, whose duty is to take no risks...

Slowly I returned to the room.

As I looked upon the table which bore the remains of our meal, I suddenly wondered whether the food we had eaten had not in fact been prepared for somebody else.

Instantly my brain seized upon this idea.

We could not have been expected: yet, if our reception was improvised, it had been amazingly done. The Baron was not in residence, yet his apartments were open and ready for use: four benighted strangers had been given a four-course dinner with more dispatch than they would have found at an inn – this notwithstanding that *so far as we were concerned* no orders had been issued to the servants until the bailiff was back from viewing the car.

The thing was clear. Company had been expected, and we had taken its place.

Before I could digest this conclusion, I saw that it was false.

If the bailiff was expecting a party, he would hardly have encouraged four strangers to usurp its lodging and board.

I felt suddenly angry with the man. As our host, he should have been friendly. Instead, he had the air of a jailer. Yes. That was right. *He had the air of a jailer…*

The word might have been a wand.

As it came into my mind, the scales fell from my eyes.

Who Baron Veners might be, I did not know. But I knew *where* he was. *And that was on his back by the side of a country road, with his hands bound fast behind him and Bell and Rowley sitting in the dark by his side.*

3

In the Enemy's Camp

As I had half expected, the bedchambers we were given were cells which the monks had used. They were very small and must have been cold in winter, for the walls and floors were of stone: but they were pleasantly furnished, and each had a little window that looked upon the courtyard.

A woman that was sewing in the passage lighted us into our rooms, and, when she had bid us 'Good night,' I entered Hanbury's chamber and shut the door.

George heard me out in silence, smoking and swinging his legs.

When I had finished –

"Good for you," he said shortly. "Once you're shown it, the thing is as clear as paint. The bailiff was expecting his master – complete with political prisoner, to wit, the heir apparent of Riechtenburg. When he saw the Grand Duchess, he guessed that the game had been bungled and smelt a chance of picking the pieces up. But the first thing to do was to see if the Duke was there: so he takes a lantern to have a look at his face. The rest's easy... But I don't think he'll send for petrol at break of day."

"I must get it," said I: "but our friend mustn't know that I've gone. So long as he thinks we suspect nothing, he'll let us alone. Sans petrol we're stuck, and he knows it. What's more, he'll swear that some's coming, to keep us glued to the house. If he asks where I am, you must say I'm keeping my bed: but, with luck, I'll be back before breakfast with Rowley and Bell."

George took his pipe from his mouth and rubbed his nose.

"Bill," says he, "don't be a fool. This dukeling may have his merits. If he has, they're damned well veiled, but they may be there. But I'll tell you this. Lump them all together and chuck in his rotten life, and they're not worth the one-night's rest of an honest man."

"I know," said I, smiling. "But I'd like to help the Grand Duchess. There's nothing the matter with her."

"I suppose this will help her," said George thoughtfully.

I shrugged my shoulders.

Then I gave him the key of the outhouse in which the Rolls stood, and told him there were arms in her locker and advised him to draw a pistol as soon as he decently could.

"And tell the Grand Duchess I've gone, but not the Duke."

"Is that wise?" said George.

"Very wise," said I. "She's a quicker wit than we have and – and better hands."

"I believe you," said George: "but she's got a whip in her boot."

I put out my candle and leaned out into the night.

There was the bailiff, still sitting by the side of the door, in case, I suppose, his master should presently come. Whether his dogs were with him, I could not tell.

I had not had much hope of being able to go that way, and, indeed, it seemed idle to have to do with the court, when the back of the house gave upon blowing meadows that ran right up to the woods. I, therefore, drew in my head and turned to the door.

Now I had learned as a child that in abbeys and suchlike foundations there was sometimes a stairway that led direct from the dormitories into the church: and it at once occurred to me that, though the church was gone, the stairway, if built in the mansion, would still be there.

A glance through my keyhole showed that the passage was in darkness, and an instant later I was stealing down it as fast as I dared. My shoes were soled with rubber and made no sound.

Sure enough, at the end of the passage I came to a winding staircase some four feet wide.

I had stopped at its head for a moment, to see if I could find handhold, in case I slipped, when I thought that I heard a movement behind my back.

I was flat against the wall in an instant, and holding my breath, but, though I stood for two minutes as still as death, the sound was not repeated, and I made up my mind that my fancy had played me a trick.

Stealthily I descended the steps.

At their foot was a little landing, and then I was brought up short by a door in the wall. Beneath this fresh air was blowing, where the aged threshold was worn.

There was neither latch nor keyhole, but only two great bolts, and these were loose in their staples, so that I was able to draw them without any noise.

At once the door swung inward, and I saw the sable country and the heaven thickset with stars.

But, if I was now free of the mansion, I was not free to be gone, for I dared not leave the door open and I could not so much as close it, when once I was out.

I could have stamped for vexation at this untimely hitch.

Had there been a latch, I would have latched it and been content. Had the oak stayed still, when I shut it, I would have left it so, and have chanced the mischief of the wind: but, as I have said, it swung inward, because it was badly hung, and I dared not leave it open, for, though no eye should see it, the draught in the passage above would tell its tale.

There was nothing to be done but go back and rouse George Hanbury. Then we could come down together and he could see me out.

Heavily I shut the door and slid a bolt back into place. Then I turned again to the stairs.

As I did so, I heard a movement two or three steps away.

In a flash I was upon the intruder, had flung an arm round his neck and had clapped a hand over his mouth.

Then I jumped like a schoolgirl, let go my prisoner and lay back against the wall.

It was the Grand Duchess.

For a moment neither of us spoke, but I know that my heart was pounding and there was sweat on my face.

At length –

"I'm most dreadfully sorry," I whispered. "I – "

"Where are you going?" she breathed.

"To Bariche for petrol. We're in the enemy's camp."

"Ah," says she. "Are you sure?"

"Certain. Hanbury will tell you tomorrow. You gave me the cue."

"Does the bailiff suspect that we know it?"

"No," said I. "And, if you'll shut this door behind me, there's no reason why he should."

"Very well."

I hesitated. Then –

"I – I must have hurt you," I stammered.

"It is nothing," she said. "How will you find your way?"

"Bariche lies South, and I can steer by the stars."

"I see," she said slowly. And then, "I don't want to fumble. You had better show me the bolts, if I am to shut the door."

She gave me her hand, and I brought her up to the door. Then, with my hands upon hers, I taught her to shoot the bolts without making a sound.

A moment later I was out on the turf, and, before five minutes were past, I had left the meadows behind and was climbing within the woods.

I have little to say of that journey, except that I can think of no error into which I did not fall.

I sought to go South, but, though the stars were luminous, I met so much mountain and forest, that my course became more ragged with every step. So sure as I found a road, this would soon curl about until I was heading North, and twice, with my eyes on the heaven, I walked clean into a ditch. I strode a mile out of my way to miss a wood, only to encounter a cliff which I could not climb, and, when, in despair, I returned and entered the wood, five minutes' scrambling brought me into a valley from which I could only escape by stumbling due East for nearly another mile. Because I could find no bridge, I stripped and forded a river to gain a road; but, before I had gone half a mile, the road turned suddenly North and over the very water I had been at such pains to cross. The countryside itself might have been enchanted. I confounded substance with shadow, and height and depth deceived me over and over again. Peer as I would, I could not judge any distance, great or small, and if ever I dared to hasten some pitfall was always ready to bring me down. If I passed by men or beasts I never saw them, while, as for habitations, I might have been wandering in some uninhabited land.

All the time I kept thinking of the Grand Duchess and our meeting upon the stair and the rough way in which I had used her before I knew that it was she. I was sure that I must have hurt her, for I am a powerful man, and, remembering the touch of her soft and yielding body and her delicate face, I cursed again the violence which I had laid on. How she had come to watch me I could not divine, but supposed that she had not known me and, finding my way suspicious, had followed me down. This seemed a poor explanation, for, when I released her, she knew me, although I had spoken no word: and that made me wonder how it was that I recognized her…

Whilst I was revolving this mystery, I caught my foot in a trailer and fell into a bramble-bush. And that was the end of my troubles, for I let out an oath so noisy that some dog began to bark, and, when I had ploughed through the briers, I saw a farm house below me and, beyond it, the white of a road.

The farmer was a decent fellow and readily agreed himself to drive me to Bariche, from which I found to my disgust I was still fourteen miles away: but, though his heart was willing and his good wife was more than kind, he did not know how to hasten, and, when I tried to teach him, began to fuss.

It follows that the day had broken long before we had taken the road, and, as this proved very hilly, by the time we came to Bariche, it was nearly seven o'clock. We drove direct to a garage, and there my luck came in, for, ere I was out of the gig, I caught sight of a card in the window which announced that some car was for sale at the price of thirty-five pounds.

Such a bargain was just what I needed, for it was now so late that I had already determined to endeavour to hire some car. Now no one would have let me a car without a driver: but, if no witness sat beside me, before I returned to the abbey I could pick up Rowley and Bell: and this I was eager to do for every reason, but especially because the longer they were left to themselves the more likely was one to go off in search of food. And that would mean a further delay; for enter Riechtenburg without them I would not, charm the Grand Duchess herself never so wisely.

The sale was not done in a moment, for, first, the car was unready, and then I had to test her before I dared drive her away. Except, however, for her battery, she seemed in pretty good trim, and I paid the price demanded at eight o'clock.

I then bought petrol and had the cans put aboard and, after rewarding the farmer, who seemed very much dumbfounded at my buying a second car, I bade them start the engine and clambered into my seat.

Be sure I had purchased a map of the largest scale I could get and had asked the name of the abbey and how I should go. The name of the place was Barabbas, which to my mind seemed proper enough, and happily the map showed it, so that I could check the directions which the farmer and others bestowed. The way was not easy to follow, but one thing was clear, namely that I could not do better than go by the scene of the struggle where I had left Rowley and Bell.

The car was not very swift, but, after the gig's progress, it seemed to be outstripping the wind, and my spirits rose, like those of a prisoner escaped, with every mile.

Very soon I came to the turning which I was to take and, a few minutes later, to the glittering glades and thickets of the forest through which we had passed.

Approaching the sunken road, I slowed down and looked about me, and almost at once I saw Bell's head and then Rowley's rise out of a press of bracken about an oak.

They had little to report.

The man I had struck had continually demanded a doctor and, when they had taken no notice, had burst into tears. Despite his misgivings, he had presently slept very sound and seemed quite relieved, upon waking, to find himself yet alive. The other had proved more unruly, for, after attempting to bribe them to let him escape, he had flown into a passion of fury, rolling about on the ground and biting the turf and then sitting up and screaming so loud that he had to be gagged. By now, however, the two were docile enough, and I think that their night in the open had quenched what spirit they had, for, when I walked over to see them, they uttered no sound, but stared at me so reproachfully that I had much ado to keep a straight face.

When I asked the servants if they had taken their arms, they showed me two heavy revolvers, too large to be easily carried or, for my part, conveniently used.

By my instructions, they then unbound their prisoners and, taking away their glazed hats, followed me back to the car: I had left the engine running, and, before the two rogues, who were stiff, had got to their feet, we were out of sight.

It seemed best to leave them there, to shift for themselves, for their borrowed plumes were against them, and I did not see what they could do but try to walk to Barabbas, avoiding, if they could, all company, lest their garb should arouse suspicions they could not lay.

I then explained the position to Rowley and Bell, and told them that, when we arrived, they were to mark the bailiff and, the moment he gave any sign of interference, to hold him up. "And mind nothing else," said I, "but him and his dogs, for he's played his hand very well and he'll be ripe for murder when he sees that he's lost the trick."

I might have spared my breath.

As, half an hour later, we entered the mouth of the valley, a full mile below the bridge, a slim figure flashed from a thicket and into the road.

I brought the car to a standstill as soon as I could.

Then –

"What's happened?" I cried.

The Grand Duchess, who was hatless, pushed back her hair.

"Grieg," she said. "Grieg has happened." She pointed back up the road. "Isn't there a track along there up which you can back?"

Bell opened the door, and she entered and sat beside me, while I took the car back fifty paces and then up a little track into cover from view.

Then I stopped the engine and waited for her to speak.

"I think one of your servants should go to keep an eye on the road."

I turned to Rowley and Bell.

49

"One," I said, "will stay at the foot of this track, and the other will go to where he can see the abbey at the end of the road. The first sign of movement, please."

They were gone in an instant, for, hungry and tired as they were, I think they loved adventure, and another brush with the major was very much to their taste.

The Grand Duchess told her tale.

"Mr Hanbury and I had breakfast at seven o'clock. Paul was not down, but the bailiff was in the courtyard. He said he had sent to Bariche and hoped the man would be back by nine o'clock. After breakfast I went to my room. I hadn't been there ten minutes, when I heard the sound of a car. Of course I thought it was you. So did Mr Hanbury, and I saw him walk out of the house with a pipe in his mouth. The car was an open car, but its hood was raised. As it swept into the court, Mr Hanbury went to meet it, and, when it was almost upon him, I saw him start. Before he could turn, 'I have you covered,' said someone. 'Stand where you are.'

"Well, of course, he was done. But he took his pipe out of his mouth and shouted 'Major Grieg' in a toast-master's voice. I didn't wait. I flew to Paul's room and woke him and told him to come with me, but of course he began to argue, so I left him and fled. I left the house by the staircase you used last night and took to the woods. My idea, of course, was to stop you from – from throwing our last card away, but I didn't dare come by the meadows – and look at my shoes."

"I will clean them," said I. I swung myself out of the car. "By the time I have done what I can, perhaps I shall have a plan."

Without a word the Grand Duchess left the car and took her seat on a log. Then she took off the slippers and gave them into my hand.

I made a wisp of fresh grass and fell to work.

I fear I thought more of the slippers than of how to outwit Major Grieg, but I think I may be forgiven, for they were very dainty and very small.

When I had cleaned them both, I knelt and shod her. Then I sat back on my heels and wiped the sweat from my face.

"And now for the plan," she said.

I fear I had expected some thanks, which, to be perfectly honest, I did not deserve, and before this sudden inquiry I felt and looked as a fool.

"It's – it's not ready yet," I said feebly.

The Grand Duchess rose to her feet and took two or three steps. Then she turned abruptly and let me see the displeasure which sat in her face.

"Then please be quick," she said coldly. "I didn't run two miles to have my shoes cleaned. If you listened to me last night, you must know there's a lot at stake."

I remember ruefully reflecting that George Hanbury was perfectly right. The lady had a whip in her boot.

The odds were clean in our favour, and, as I drove over the bridge, I knew in my heart that, if Fortune kept out of the ring, the round was ours.

I was alone in the car, and this was moving slowly and making a shocking noise. To round the picture, as I approached the abbey, I sounded the horn...

The court was empty and full of the glare of the sun, and the open doorway of the mansion looked like a square, black mouth.

As I came to the edge of the court, the car gave a sickening jerk and then stopped dead, with her radiator steaming and hissing as though it was ready to burst.

For a moment I sat where I was. Then I got out slowly and lugged two cans of petrol out of the back of the car.

With one in each hand I hastened towards the out-house, which lay behind the refectory towards the woods. It follows that within five seconds *I was out of sight of the mansion and of anyone watching from within.*

51

Out of sight, I ran for the corner and, when I had turned it, I set my cans in position and lay back against the wall.

Immediately opposite me, about six paces away, Bell was behind a chestnut, and, though I could not see Rowley, I knew that he was at hand.

We had not long to wait.

Grieg came running delicately, as a man who will lose no time yet make no noise.

Round the corner he pelted and, meeting the stumbling-block which I had set up, took such a fall as I have never seen except in a cinema-show.

I was kneeling astride him in an instant, and, though he let off his pistol, he must have fired into the ground, for he was lying face downwards and I had hold of his wrist.

I had expected a struggle, for I knew he was brave, but, as I have said, he was heavy, and such a fall as his would have shaken a feather-weight. Be that as it may, when I told him to drop his pistol, he did so without a word. Then I brought his arms behind him, and Rowley bound together his wrists.

I rose to see his chauffeur standing against the wall and gazing upon Bell's pistol with his eyes starting out of his head.

It was easy to take his measure.

"Go and call the bailiff," said I. "Say that the major sent you. Understand that. The major sent you. If he isn't here in one minute, I'll follow and take your life."

Bell put up his pistol, and the fellow was off like a hare.

When I looked again at Grieg, he had not stirred, so the servants turned him over and I unfastened his tunic about his throat. At this, he opened his eyes, to dart me a look of such malevolence that I saw he was more sulky than sick and let him be.

As I stood upright, I saw the Grand Duchess standing twenty paces away. It was plain that she had been running, for she held her hand to her side and was out of breath.

At once I pointed to the chestnut, and she darted behind its trunk. As she did so, the bailiff came running, with his dogs before him and the chauffeur halting behind.

Before he had reached the corner, I stepped out and held him up.

"If you value your dogs," said I, "you'll call them to heel."

In a sense, it was a bow at a venture: but I wanted to spare the dogs and I thought that, if he was fond of them, he would probably see the wisdom of not putting up a resistance which they would be sure to abet.

As luck would have it, I seemed to have done the right thing, for he called them hoarsely by name and I saw his fingers trembling, as he made to seize their collars and hold them fast.

Leaving Rowley with Grieg, we others returned to the house.

It was a curious procession that presently crossed the court – the bailiff bent well-nigh double, to keep his hold on his dogs, the chauffeur skulking behind him with his hands in the air, as much afraid of the bailiff as of what was behind, Bell, imperturbable as ever and looking remarkably spruce, and I, very hot and dusty and something ashamed of a victory which had been so easily won.

As we approached the mansion, the Duke looked out of a window upon the first floor.

"Hullo," he said.

"Where's Hanbury?" said I.

"I don't know," he said. "I'm locked in."

George was fast in a closet that opened out of the parlour in which we had dined: and, since he had proved it a prison out of which, without tools, you could not possibly break, when we had brought him out, we ushered the bailiff in.

"Grieg all right?" said George. "Not that I care particularly. He's got a nasty mind."

"I'm just going to get him," said I. I pointed to the chauffeur. "The Duke's upstairs, under key. Will you let him out and lock up this wallah instead? If we put him with Grieg or the bailiff, they'll break his neck."

"And my lady?" says George.

"This is her show," said I. "I should have bought it as you did, if she hadn't stepped out of a thicket two miles away."

With that, I called Bell and left George rubbing his nose…

I found Grieg nursing his fury, as a pot full of water that simmers upon the fire.

When I bade him rise, he would not, but when the servants would have raised him, he shook them off.

I fingered my chin.

"It's no pleasure to them to touch you: but, if you don't want to be handled, you'd better do as you're told."

Somehow he got to his feet and stood shaking with rage.

"Next time, by God," he said thickly, and left it there.

"Put him with the bailiff," said I, and they marched him off.

I watched them wheel into the court. Then I turned to the chestnut tree.

"You promised," I said, "to stay in the woods till I sent."

The Grand Duchess came forth.

"I know," she said. "Who – who was it that fired?"

"Grieg's pistol went off," I said curtly.

The Grand Duchess stopped in her tracks.

"I will not be spoken to like that."

"And I will not have promises broken," I said steadily.

The Grand Duchess came to me quietly and stood looking into my face with fire in her eyes. I hope I met her gaze squarely.

"How dare you?" she breathed.

"Because I'm right," said I. "I said that I wouldn't move, unless you gave me your word. I was right to exact that promise. This twopenny rough and tumble might have gone wrong."

"What if it had?"

"You would have been safe," said I.

"I don't value my safety."

"I know that," said I.

My lady shrugged her shoulders and glanced at her wrist.

"Time's getting on," she said. "I hate to ask you, but, if you would drive us to Vigil…"

I turned on my heel and left her without a word.

The tyres of the car Grieg had used were of the same size as ours, so, when Rowley and Bell had eaten, they took out three of his tubes to replace the three of ours which the snags had pricked. Then they took his sparking-plugs and those of the car I had bought, so that both the cars were disabled and could only be moved by hand. While they were doing these things, George was pouring the petrol into the tank of the Rolls, and I was scouring the stables for one of the farmer's men.

At last a maidservant told me that these were all in the fields, except the groom we had seen the night before, and that he had withdrawn to the cellar on hearing the shot.

"Tell him he'll hear another, if he doesn't come up."

The man came in fear which he took no pains to conceal. But I think he was something dull and the strangeness of the proceedings had disordered his wits.

When I had reassured him, I showed him the keys of the closet and the bedroom where the chauffeur was shut.

"Your master," I said, "would be very glad of these keys. But I haven't done with them yet. So I'm going to take you with me – for a ten-mile run. Then I'll hand them over to you and you can walk back."

Whilst I was speaking, the Rolls stole into the court.

"At last," said the Duke, getting up from the cloister's bench and throwing to some pigeons the end of his cigarette. "Was that your last cigarette?"

"Yes," said I.

"Oh, hell," says he. "I wish I could smoke a pipe."

With that, he climbed into the car.

When I told the groom to follow –

"What's this?" said the Duke.

"My orders," said I shortly.

He looked black enough at that, but said no more.

I bade the servants get in and the groom stand between them and hold to the backs of their chairs.

When the Grand Duchess did not appear, I told George to sound the horn.

He did so, and, after a little, he did so again.

The Duke lifted up his voice.

"Leonie!" he bawled. "Leonie!"

There was no reply, and, after waiting a minute, I entered the house quickly and passed upstairs.

The doors of the cells were open, except, of course, that behind which the chauffeur lay, but, though I looked into each, they were empty enough.

As I stood in the passage, frowning, a cool draught of air made itself felt...

At once I ran to the stair at the farther end and, hardly knowing why I did so, began to descend the steps.

The Grand Duchess was standing in the doorway that gave to the fields, leaning against the old jamb, with her eyes on the sunlit meadows, as though she was deep in thought.

"The – the car is ready," I said.

She neither spoke nor turned, but she put out a little hand.

I do not think the man is born that could have withstood such a gesture of such a maid.

I know I came to her quickly and put her hand to my lips.

Then I looked up to meet her eyes.

"I think you must hate me," she said.

In that moment my world was changed.

Everything I knew and cared for – my friends, my home, my horses, the open air and the sunlight, all that made up my life seemed suddenly dependent for their value upon her smile.

"Oh, my dear," I said, and could have bitten my tongue.

She did not seem to see my confusion, for she had lowered her eyes, and, on a sudden impulse, again I kissed her hand.

I looked up to find her smiling.

"You take refuge in deeds," she said.

Then she put her hands behind her and leaned back against the wall.

"Paul's not out of the wood," she said quietly. "Even at Vigil he won't be out of the wood. Not until he is proclaimed. And in need I – we have no one to help us as you have done. Supposing…where could I find you?"

"At Vigil," said I. "You shall have the address tonight."

She stood very still.

"I – I didn't mean that," she said.

"I know. I'd like to be – in the background."

"I – I didn't mean that either," she said.

"I know that," said I.

She turned and looked over the meadows and up at the bluff.

"Will you promise to be careful?" she said. And then, "I heard what Grieg said."

"I will do anything you ask me," I said unsteadily.

The Grand Duchess drew in her breath.

"Just now you spoke of the background… If I let you stay in the background – would you…understand?"

"Yes," said I.

She looked round swiftly.

"Perhaps you will – one day," she said.

4

At the Sign of 'The Square of Carpet'

I suppose I had heard of Vigil, but I had never met one who had been there or seen, so far as I remember, its name in print: and, while that is nothing to go by, for I am not well informed, I have since referred to the guide-books to find the city dismissed with half a line. This is to me a mystery, for, though, perhaps, of little importance, Vigil is more attractive than many a well-known resort, and I can only suppose that the singular absence of any kind of hotel has stifled again and again its claim to renown.

The town lies among mountains upon either side of a river which flows very swift, and, if you approach from the East, you will suddenly see it beneath you, spread out like a map and resembling those fabulous cities that painters raised in their backgrounds five hundred years ago.

Now, when we first saw it, George and I were afoot, as well as alone, and so were able to loiter as long as we pleased.

The Rolls had gone on to Vigil, with the servants upon her front seat. I had thought this arrangement a wise one, and George had agreed. Four miles from the city, therefore, the change had been made, and, almost before our guests knew it, the servants had taken our places, and we were out in the road.

The Duke sat still, but the Grand Duchess started up with a little cry.

"I beg you'll excuse us," I said, with my hat in my hand. "It's better so. The less attention attracted, the fewer the questions asked."

"If you want another reason," said George, "Chandos dislikes the limelight, until he has shaved."

The Grand Duchess smiled.

"I expect you know best," she said. "I don't know how we happened to fall into such good hands. Goodbye – for the moment."

"So long," said the Duke casually. "An' many thanks. What do you want for this car?"

"She's not for sale," said Hanbury.

Then I nodded to Bell, and the Rolls slid forward.

When the dust had settled, we walked down the road in its wake and presently came to the standpoint which, had we not been afoot, we should not have enjoyed.

I have said that the town was below us, and so it was: but it was four miles distant, so that we had by no means a bird's eye view. The air, however, was clear, as is the air of those parts, and the red and grey roofs and buildings stood out very sharp and pleasing, with the brilliant blue of the river cutting them across like a sash.

We at once perceived the cathedral, thrusting two massive towers, and a building by the side of the river which must, we thought, be the palace, for there were trees about it and open space. Four bridges spanned the river, one of them covered and crooked and so, I suppose, very old, and far to the North we could make out a big parade-ground upon which we could see quite plainly the flash of steel.

Here let me say what I should have set down before this – that the moment we came to the frontier we knew that the Prince was not dead, for the flags were mast-head high, and, though we asked no questions, it was everywhere perfectly plain that nothing unusual had occurred.

At last I turned from the city and looked at George.

"I should like to stay at Vigil," I said. "The servants can go to Salzburg and fetch our things."

"Very well," said George slowly. "I've only one thing against it, and that's Duke Paul. Not that he'll trouble us: he was plainly immensely relieved when we got out of the car. But I should like to forget him. Intercourse with that youth is like drinking a glass of cheap claret which is badly corked. Long live Prince Nicholas."

"I'm with you," said I. "If the old fellow dies, we'll leave Vigil the very next day."

"Once he's proclaimed," said George. "Did you promise to stay till then?"

"Practically," said I.

George nodded approvingly.

"She's out of the top drawer," he said. "I'd like to see her on Flattery, with scent breast high and the merchant making for Bulrush by way of The Dale. Why the devil is she backing this waster?"

"You can search me," said I, and meant it.

For a little we smoked in silence, regarding the distant city, so gay in the sun.

"I can't understand it," said George violently. "Of course she loathes him – that's nothing. The girl he found in the chorus loathed the sound of his voice. He is – loathsome. Very well. Loathsome or not, she's got to marry him. Why? Because she's the obvious person to play the Princess. If you want another reason, she's the head of the second line. She's betrothed to the heir apparent, not to the man. She goes with the throne."

"I agree," said I heartily.

"Then why the blazes doesn't she let him rip? Let him work out his own damnation and *lose his throne*?"

"And marry Johann?" said I.

"Johann's married," said George. "I looked at the Almanach last night."

If her attitude troubled George, it confounded me.

The girl had no wish to be Princess. She had said so before us all, and no one that heard her say it could doubt that she meant what she said. *She detested the Duke*. Upon her chastisement of him I lay no stress: a woman can dissemble her love. But spirits of her sort do not like spirits of his. The thought of becoming his wife must be plain horror.

These two premises admitted, she had everything to gain by inaction and nothing to lose.

By folding her hands at Anger, she might well have escaped a future to her more repulsive than death. Yet she had come out to fight…

The matter passed my understanding, and I would very gladly have put it out of my mind: but this I could not do, and that for a reason which I think I have made plain enough.

George Hanbury was speaking, as though to himself.

" 'Vanity of Vanities,' " he said slowly. " 'All is vanity.' And that's a peach of a watchword for a couple of fools who are going to Vanity Fair."

"One fool," said I quickly.

"Two," said George. "If I had any sense, I should take you back to Maintenance – if necessary, by force."

We lunched very well and simply beneath the awning of a tavern in the heart of the town. Far above us the bells of the cathedral rang with a pleasing jingle each quarter of the hour: on the roof of an aged house we could see a stork, like a sentry, beside his nest: an apothecary's faced us, with monks behind the old counter and a Latin superscription above the door, and next to this stood a handsome white-stone cinema-house, whose boards announced a film which was being shown in London two months before.

In the streets, which were old and paved, yokes of oxen went plodding by the side of open taxis as silent of movement as themselves, and peasants, clad in white linen and wearing embroidered sashes and waistcoats laced with gold, were mingling with men and women whose attire would have passed unremarked in the Place Vendôme.

Later, when we went strolling, we found these curious conditions on every side. Ancient and modern fashions seemed to thrive knee to knee, and primitive styles and manners were neighboured by others which might have come straight from Paris the day before.

When, however, we sought an hotel, there was none to be found, and a man we accosted advised us to go to the station, if we had need of a bed. Thither we accordingly went, but the lodging offered us was shameful, and I would sooner have slept on the riverside.

We then returned to the tavern where we had lunched and asked the host to recommend us an inn, but to our dismay he immediately mentioned the station as affording the only shelter which we could possibly use. When we protested, the fellow threw up his hands. Vigil, he declared, had boasted two handsome hotels before the Great War: as luck would have it, the one vying with the other, each had been wholly refitted in 1914 – this at prodigious expense which the custom sure to be attracted was to defray: instead of increasing their custom, the black years which followed had taken even that which they had and had brought them both to ruin, so that one was now the War Office and the other had been turned into flats. There were inns, he said, for the peasants, but at these we should find no bedding nor so much as a private room, and, though there was always the monastery, the discipline there was a byword, and at nine o'clock of the evening the doors were shut.

This unexpected setback disordered our simple plans, for, our personal comfort apart, we were especially anxious not to attract attention and had, to that end, decided to make no use of the Rolls, but to lay her up in some garage until we should need her again. Now, however, it seemed that, since there was no room in Vigil, we should have to leave the city and put up at some country inn and – what was far worse – go to and fro daily, because the Grand Duchess was expecting that I should be within call. The more I considered such a shift, the less I liked it, and I was wondering desperately whether we could find a house-agent and hire some flat or apartment for two or three weeks, when the landlord, who had left us staring, came back and ventured to ask us whether we were proposing to make some considerable stay.

George shrugged his shoulders.

"Man proposes, but Vigil disposes," he said. "How the devil can we stay in a city which harbours no guests?"

The man nodded over his shoulder.

"Sir," said he, "a particular friend of mine has this moment come in. He is butler to a gentleman who has a very fine flat. His wife is the cook. His master is away just now, and the flat is to let."

"By all means produce him," said George.

The man was quiet to look at and well-behaved. When we asked if the flat had been placed in some agent's hands, he replied that his master had left the matter to him, because there was but one agent and him he disliked. He had, he said, full authority, provided that he and his wife remained as butler and cook and the rent was paid in advance, a month at a time.

The tale was easy to tell, and I think we both suspected that here was a faithless servant betraying a master's trust, but, for what it was worth, we decided to see the flat and, hailing a passing taxi, we drove there at once.

The flat was upon the ground floor of a fine, three-storied mansion which rose upon the bank of the river within its own ground. By its side stood a big garage, divided, like the house, into three, one third, as the butler vouchsafed, belonging to each of the flats. Though it had not been built as a flat, the apartment was most convenient and made our rooms at Salzburg seem very rough. It was well and comfortably furnished with a lot of leather and oak, and some very pleasant etchings hung on the walls.

When we asked what was the rent, the servant named a figure which seemed to us fair, and, indeed, we would have paid more, for the place was just what we wanted and there were a butler and cook to take the cares of housekeeping out of our hands: but, though we were ready to agree, we could not help thinking of Maintenance and how we should blame a stranger that accepted the word of our servants that he could make use of our home.

Whilst we were hesitating, the butler divined our thoughts and, speaking very civilly, suggested that we should visit the Riechtenburg Bank, "for," said he, "that is my master's Bank, and anyone there will tell you that I have authority to act upon his behalf."

That was enough for us, and George sat down at a table and drew up a rough Agreement which the three of us signed, and, though we had not enough money to pay a month's rent then and there, the butler said that that did not matter and asked if he should serve dinner at eight o'clock.

I will not dwell on our good fortune, for I think it speaks for itself; but I must confess that it lifted a weight from my mind, for it is one thing to commit a friend to a thankless venture, but another to condemn him to discomfort which the giving up of your venture would automatically relieve.

We then returned to the garage where we had left the Rolls and gave the servants the orders which we had composed.

Rowley was to leave for Salzburg, to fetch our luggage, at once. Travelling by train, he would be back at Vigil at five the next day. Bell was to take a note to the Grand Duchess – addressed, of course, to the house at which he had set her down and containing a sheet of the notepaper which we had found in the flat – and, when it was dark, to bring the Rolls to its garage and then report to us that this had been done.

By the time we were back in the fiat it was half past four, and within five minutes I was asleep in a loggia which was overlooking the river and might have been a pleasance of Morpheus himself.

It was ten o'clock that evening, before Bell came to report.

As he entered the room, the bell of the telephone rang.

It was the Grand Duchess speaking.

"Listen," she said. "How soon will you have your things?"

"Tomorrow," said I, "in the course of the afternoon."

"Then will you both dine with me – tomorrow, at nine o'clock? Or do you never dine?"

"If you please," said I, "we should like to break our rule."

"Good night," said the Grand Duchess, and put her receiver back.

When I had told George Hanbury, I turned to Bell.

"Everything all right?" I said.

"Yes, sir," he said. "The car's under lock and key."

"Well, you turn in," said I. "You've earned your rest."

"Very good, sir," said Bell. He hesitated. "If I should hear any movements, am I to let you know?"

George and I looked at him.

"Any movements?" said George, laying his paper down.

"Such as a car, sir," said Bell. "I mean, if Major Grieg wants to, he could be here before dawn."

"But why should he want to?" said I. "Besides, if he did, for the moment we've covered our tracks."

Bell looked from me to George. Then he moistened his lips.

"Excuse me, sir," he said, "but I thought you must know. *Major Grieg has the flat above this. I carried his letters upstairs five minutes ago.*"

At ten minutes to nine the next evening George and I mounted the steps of a house in the Lessing Strasse, a short, quiet street, full of lime-trees, and running down to the river, not far from the palace itself.

Before we had time to ring, the door was opened, and we were presently ushered into a high-pitched salon, well and delicately furnished after the style of Louis XVI.

The Grand Duchess rose to greet us, looking more lovely than ever, so very white were her shoulders and so shapely her slim, bare arms.

At once she introduced us to the Countess Dresden of Salm, "who is really your hostess," she said, "for you will eat her dinner and this is her house; but she lets me call it my party, because she has always spoiled me, ever since I was her bridesmaid six years ago."

The Countess laughed.

"How many people in Vigil," she said, "would jump at the chance?"

She was young and very good-looking and had a most charming smile, and I set her down at once as the wife of some high official, accustomed to entertaining and to playing a gracious part.

"There's one other guest," said the Grand Duchess: "and that, I'm afraid, is a man; but he very much wants to meet you and thank you for all you've done. He's the Lord President of the Council and almost the only courtier we really trust. You see, I hide nothing from you and I want you to know where we stand. His name is Sully – the Baron Sully, if you like."

Here the door was opened, and the man of whom she was speaking was ushered into the room.

It was our sometime tutor.

I looked round dazedly.

Madame Dresden was openly laughing, and the Grand Duchess was smiling at Hanbury, who was standing with his mouth open and a hand to his head.

Sully greeted the ladies. Then he laid his hands on our shoulders and held us fast.

"I am told," he said, "that your German does me credit: that you both speak fluently, Hanbury with a fine carelessness, and Chandos with a rugged sincerity which knows no law."

"Oh, what a shame!" cried the Grand Duchess. "And I never put it like that."

But we were all laughing, for the description was as faithful as witty, as all of us knew.

Not until dinner was over was reference made to the matters which had led us to Riechtenburg.

Then the Grand Duchess looked at Sully, who sat on her right.

"How is the Prince?" she said.

"He is like the master of a ship, your Highness, in waters in which no ship can live. He carries on according to the best traditions, but the next big wave will be the end of him. Till then – well, he held a Council this afternoon."

"And Johann?"

"Duke Johann gives rise to anxiety. As you know, he is Colonel-in-Chief of the Black Hussars. As such, he must do duty with them for one month in each year. Well, he has selected this month. Whilst we were talking yesterday, the matter was being rushed through. It appeared in Orders last night, and this morning he took up his command. He is on duty now – at the palace."

"At the palace?" cried the Countess.

"At the palace," said Sully. "Today is the first of July. Today at noon the Black Hussars were due to relieve the Greys. They will be there until September, when they in their turn will be relieved."

The Grand Duchess set down her glass.

"He commands the Praetorian Guard."

"I hope not," said Sully. "But every soldier in and about the palace will normally do as he says."

The Grand Duchess drew in her breath.

"It's an act of war, Baron."

Sully raised his eyebrows.

"Unhappily, your Highness, that is a matter of opinion. We consider it such. But one paper says, 'In view of HRH's indisposition, Duke Johann's decision to command his regiment during its arduous term of duty as Body Guard is a particularly graceful act.' "

"He's very clever," said my lady musingly. "What can we do?"

"Not very much," said Sully. "Sahreb has been told to go sick and Kneller has been wired for to take his place."

"As lord-in-waiting?"

"Yes. But Kneller is a general upon the active list. He is, therefore, the Duke's superior officer and could, for instance, put him under arrest."

I think we all started, for Sully was not the man to use such words lightly, and violence of any sort was foreign to his soul.

"Does the Prince know?" said the Countess.

Sully nodded.

"When I told HRH, he laughed. 'Wheresoever the carcase is,' he said. Then he sent for Duke Johann and thanked him heartily. 'I am much touched, Johann. On your last day of duty I shall be photographed with the field-officers of the Guard. Sully, you will remind me.' The Duke did what he could to express his thanks. When he was gone, the Prince laughed till he coughed. Nothing will make him believe that his hour is at hand."

There was a little silence.

Then –

"Grieg has resigned his Commission," continued Sully. "At least the *Gazette* says so, and I don't imagine he'll say the *Gazette* is wrong. I'd have liked to put him out of the country: but he wouldn't take that lying down."

"I'm disappointed," said the Grand Duchess. "Grieg ought to be broken – and to drag Johann down in his fall."

"That is a scandal," said Sully, "which I would cheerfully face. But a charge of treason is a very high explosive, and, as such, we cannot use it, except to shatter the Duke. And we've no evidence against him."

"Grieg?"

"Never," said Sully. "All the hope he has is in *Prince* Johann."

"And the others the same?"

"Undoubtedly," said Sully. "Besides, their bare word would be useless. And so would Grieg's. And I hardly think it likely that they have their orders in writing for what they have done."

"Not their orders," said George. We all looked at him. "But Grieg's not the man to risk being double-crossed. I don't know about the others, but I'll bet he's got some writing which Duke Johann will have to redeem if he comes to the throne."

The Grand Duchess returned to Sully.

"Mr Hanbury's right," she said. "Grieg would never trust Johann. What's more, scandal or no, Grieg ought to be under arrest."

I confess I agreed with her. Grieg had received his sentence, and – a man may as well be hanged for a sheep as a lamb. What was still more to the point, if Johann came to the throne, the sentence would be revoked.

Sully looked very grave.

"The inevitable court-martial, your Highness, would have been momentous. Counsel would have been engaged: Duke Paul would have had to appear. It was felt that it would be improper to subject his Highness Duke Paul to such an ordeal."

"Ah," said the Grand Duchess softly, and that was all.

Her little exclamation showed me the truth.

Court-martial Grieg, and Duke Paul must be cross-examined. That was a prospect his supporters dared not face.

The horrid irony of the business filled my mind. At every turn it was Duke Paul himself that put a spoke in his wheel. Great hearts were fighting his battle – with the man and all his works like a millstone about their neck.

"Still," said Sully, "I am hoping that Grieg is an empty gun – a gun that has been fired and cannot, lest it burst in the hand, be fired again. Meanwhile, I am very thankful that your Highness is here. Since the news became known, there has been a marked rush to book seats for Wednesday night."

The Grand Duchess turned to me.

"It is the Prince's birthday, and a gala performance will be given in the opera house. *Tosca*. Paul and I have got to be on parade."

"Such parades," said Sully, "are invaluable. I trust you will persuade his Highness to appear with you tomorrow at the polo and on Tuesday at the Fête of St Anatole."

The Grand Duchess raised her eyebrows.

"I'll do what I can," she said.

Then she glanced at the Countess and the five of us rose.

When the door had closed behind the two women, Sully returned to the table and lighted a cigarette.

"I became your tutor," he said, "when Duke Paul's father had renounced his right to the throne. I felt very strongly that his renunciation should not be accepted, that every effort should be made to induce him to think again. But the Prince was angry, very naturally very angry. A man, he said, that put his hand to the plough and then looked back was not fit for the kingdom of man. When I opposed him, he told me to take the same road... Perhaps he was right. No one will ever know that. But, when he fell sick, he recalled me. As you know, I left you and came. 'Why did you oppose me?' he said... I told him because I had mistrusted the Duke Johann."

"You saw further," said George.

"In politics," said Sully, "there are two kinds of sight – near sight and long sight. Neither is satisfactory. The Prince has one and I have the other, and heaven only knows which is the best. At the present moment I wish that I had his eyes, for I cannot see my way clearly, and he, as I have told you, has his fast shut."

George looked at me over the rim of his glass.

"Sister Anne, what do you see?"

"The palace guard," said I, "must be changed."

"That," said Sully, "is impossible."

"Then the Prince must be moved."

"The physicians are against it," said Sully, "and the Prince himself would refuse."

"Then," said I, "the Prince must contrive to live until August the first."

"And I'll back the lady," said George. "Duke Paul must be dummy, and the Grand Duchess play the hands. Out and about the place from morning to night. The theatre, polo, shopping. But he must be in the picture."

Sully seemed to wince.

"He is very difficult," he said. "Grieg's attempt has sorely shaken his nerve."

"Naturally," said George quietly. And then, "You mean he keeps house?"

"Yes."

"The police?"

"The police are wolves in sheep's clothing, so far as he is concerned."

"I see," said George, frowning. "If he felt safe, would he go when and where he was told?"

"Not always," said Sully.

"Then he must have reason to think that, when he is out with her Highness, he is safer than anywhere else."

Sully sat back in his chair.

"Bring that about," he said warmly, "and you add five years to my life."

"Easy enough," said George, and turned to me. "Duke Paul trusts Bell and Rowley, and we're not using the Rolls. Put the three at her disposal – not his."

"With the greatest pleasure," said I.

George returned to Sully.

"The Duchess had a nice Rolls-Royce,

With chauffeurs white as snow,

And everywhere the Duchess went,

The Duke was sure to go."

Sully rose to his feet, with shining eyes.

"Kingmaker," he said.

A gramophone was playing in the salon, and Caruso's *Pagliacci* was floating into the night, but, when the song was over, the Grand Duchess called for light music and Sully changed the records while the rest of us danced.

"So I am to have your car," said the Grand Duchess over my shoulder.

"It was Hanbury's brain-wave," said I.

"And to play the fine lady, while you and he – "

"You are the fine lady," said I.

"For my sins," she said shortly.

With that, she stopped dancing and led the way to a terrace that gave upon a garden shrouded with trees.

"I am very much depressed," she said quietly. "Paul sulks in his cabin, and Johann has seized the bridge. My strutting on the promenade-deck can't balance matters like that."

"Tomorrow," said I, "I very much hope that Duke Paul will go out and about."

"Perhaps – thanks to you. But Paul is not Prince Charming. He does not inspire a loyalty which will weather a *coup d'état*."

I could not bear to see her troubled, but I could think of no comfort that I could give.

Sully and George seemed to bend their eyes on the people, but I could see no further than the palace and the sentries about its gates. Already Johann as good as possessed the throne, and someone has said that possession is nine points of the law. To be sure, the Prince still lived, but the danger was imminent. Council-chamber, throne room, post-office – all were in Johann's hands. At a nod from Johann, admission could and would be denied to Sully himself. As for Duke Paul…

"I am slow," I said suddenly. "I cannot see the way out. But I will try to find it, for I know it is there."

"This is not Barabbas," said she.

"I know. That was very easy."

"You made it seem so," she said. She pulled a rose from a pillar and put it up to her lips. "What is your plan this time?"

"I have none," I cried. "I tell you, I – "

"Try to think of one now."

Desperately I covered my eyes. But I could think of nothing but the beautiful thing beside me with the pretty flower to her mouth.

As I lifted my head –

"Shall I leave you?" said the Grand Duchess.

I thought that she was smiling, but, because we stood in the shadows, I could not be sure.

"If I am to think of others, I fear your Highness must go."

The Grand Duchess stood very still.

"You must not call me 'Your Highness,' " she said quietly. "It – it does not suit you."

"I will not do it again."

With a sudden movement she put the rose to my lips.

"Marya has the sweetest roses," she said. "Their perfume is like a message that cannot be put into words."

I could only nod.

She took back the blossom and, after a moment, pinned it against her dress.

"Let us go back and dance," she said.

George and I walked to our flat, for the night was lovely and we were glad of the stroll.

By one consent we had said nothing of Grieg, for, except that we knew where he dwelt, we had nothing to say, and the Grand Duchess would have been troubled to think that he and we were now living cheek by jowl.

The man had returned that evening, not long before we went out – to judge from the slam of his door, in an ugly mood. What he would do, when he learned that we were his neighbours, I should have been glad to know, for I could not make up my mind whether it was good or evil for each of such enemies to have the other under his eye.

My wish was granted before the hour was out.

Bell had admitted us, and we had just told him the new duty which he and Rowley were to do, when we heard a car in the drive.

In a flash we were at a window commanding that side of the house, to see a taxi at rest at the foot of the steps.

No one alighted, but after a moment or two we heard the slam of Grieg's door.

That the fellow had ordered the taxi was now very plain, and I had little doubt that he had made some appointment which was better not kept by day. It seemed a pity, if we could, not to hear the address…

The engine of the taxi was running, and the car was facing away from where we stood.

George opened the window swiftly, and I was out in an instant and lying flat in the flowerbed which flanked the steps. As I took a deep breath, Grieg came out of the house.

"*The Square of Carpet,*" he said thickly, and entered the car.

George had a directory ready before I was back in the flat.

"*The Square of Carpet,*" said I. "I guess it's a kind of night-club, but we may as well see."

"Temple or pot-house," said George, "I'll bet it contains Johann. Grieg's taken the knock pretty badly and he wants to be sure that his principal's not getting cold. I don't suppose Johann wants to see him, but Grieg's not the sort of ladder that you can kick down. And, as Grieg can't go to the palace and Johann daren't come here, they meet in some market to which every-one can go."

The Square of Carpet was a café not very far from the cathedral, and less than half an hour's walk from where we stood: since it was dark, however, we took the Rolls and, alighting by the cathedral, told Bell to drive her home and, when he had put her away, to go to bed.

The streets were poorly lighted, and we could not make out their names, but a policeman whom we accosted pointed to the mouth of an alley and bade us turn to the left. We did as he said, and as we turned the corner, we heard a faint sound of music and saw ahead a cluster of red and yellow lights.

We were now in a street of great age. It was so narrow that no big car could have used it, and as if that were not enough, the houses on either hand had been built out above the pavement and were in some places so near that a man leaning out of a window could have handed a basket to another on the opposite side.

A man was ahead of us, wrapped in a voluminous cloak, and we saw him turn under an archway above which the lights I have mentioned were making a paltry show. We therefore quickened our steps and reached the archway in time to see him enter a pretentious but shabby hall, a place of high lights and dirty paintwork, with a gorgeous crimson carpet which had been trodden into holes. A seedy attendant in livery offered to take his cloak, but, when the man ignored him, another swung open a door whose mirror was cracked, and the man passed in.

We followed immediately.

The place was very much bigger than I had supposed.

A dancing floor was ringed by a promenade, and this was surrounded by boxes of which there were two tiers. A band was playing lustily, and the floor was full, but the women were wearing their day clothes and, while there were plenty of uniforms, I only saw one man wearing evening dress.

Almost at once some official was bowing before us and proposing to assign us a box, and, since it seemed best to take one, we told him to lead the way.

A vile, dark flight of stairs brought us up to the second tier, at the back of which lay a passage some three feet wide. Along this we passed for so long that I was about to protest when our guide flung open a door and ushered us into a box which was almost facing the entrance from which we had come. Then he shut the door and left us without a word.

"That means champagne," said George.

Sure enough a waiter arrived before we had had time to look round and opened a bottle of wine with a great deal of fuss.

We paid what he asked and told him to bring some beer. At this he seemed astonished and stared at the wine, but, when we repeated our order, he shrugged his shoulders and went.

A glance around suggested that we were wasting our time.

Grieg was not on the floor or the promenade, and since the boxes were dark, he had only to draw back his chair to be out of view. Most of them, indeed, appeared empty, till the sparkle of a glass being raised betrayed an occupant, and I reflected rather dismally that, if we had paused to consider, we might have known what to expect. Still, the fellow was there somewhere, and so, I was sure, was Johann, and we felt that to go would be foolish, when by staying we might see something which we could turn to our use another day. So we hung up our coats and sat down and wished for the beer.

The heat was awful, and the air was most thick and foul. There can have been no vent-holes and there were certainly no fans. A dense haze of tobacco smoke filled every corner like a fog.

"What we need," said George, "is a guide – some wallah that frequents this place and cadges his drinks."

As he spoke, the door of the box was opened, and a girl put in her head.

"Talk of the devil," said George, and called her in.

She entered with her companion – as pitiful a thing as herself, and George began to entertain them, whilst I poured out some champagne.

One was French, so I was presently able to do my share, and George played up to the other in a masterly way.

Very soon he asked them to point out to us Duke Paul, but at once they said that he was not there that night and that, when his fiancée was in Vigil, she would not let him go out.

"Who is his fiancée?" said George.

"Leonie," was the answer. "She hates the sight of him."

"Nonsense," said George.

"Of course she does," said the girl. "When he's kissed her hand she washes it in Lysol within the hour."

"Then why does she keep him at home?"

"For her pride," said the girl. "Leonie's proud as heaven. You ought to try to see her. She's like the queens they put in a picture-book."

"Well, she'll be one one day," said George.

The girl shrugged her shoulders.

"Some say Paul wants to renounce. If he did, it'd let in his cousin. He's here tonight, but he never comes out of his box."

"Which is his box?" said George.

"I don't know," said the girl. "I don't know what he comes for. I've never had a drink off him yet."

"I think he's gone," said the other, regarding her empty glass. "Don't you two like champagne?"

"Not very much," said I, and filled her glass.

"Why don't they bring that beer?" said George. "If I don't have something to drink, my lungs'll seize."

"There's a bell somewhere," said the French girl, stifling a yawn.

I found the bell and rang it with all my might. Conversation began to wane. We tried to steer it back to the royal house, but our guests seemed weary of the subject and every approach to it was greeted listlessly.

"Who's that?" said George suddenly. "Going out by the door?"

His informant pulled off her hat and shook back her hair.

77

"What? Where?" she said casually, leaning forward. "Oh, that's Johann. Seems to be rowing someone. Oh, my word, it's the Bear."

Cautiously we peered from our cover, to see a tall man in blue, with a lean and hungry look and a close-clipped moustache. His air was imperious, and his collar and cuffs, like Duke Paul's, were laced with gold. Grieg stood before him, lowering, and the other was rating him sharply for all to see. As we watched, his chin went up in a final toss, and, leaving Grieg standing silent, he swaggered out of the place.

It was a theatrical exit, and I was sure that the scene had been planned between them to demolish any rumour that they were at one. It certainly created a sensation, for the dancing was almost at a standstill, and people were crowding to the doorway and standing up in the boxes and craning their necks. About Grieg himself the press was especially thick, but he seemed to take no notice, and though two officers were asking him something or other, he made no answer but only looked very black.

Here something fell against me, and when I looked round I found a girl's head on my shoulder, heavy as lead.

I was not in the mood for advances of such a kind, but I did not want to be churlish, so I made some jest or other and asked her to have some more wine.

To my surprise she neither moved nor answered, and an instant later I found that she was asleep.

I immediately turned to the other to call her attention to her friend; but her head was down on the table and she was sleeping like the dead.

I looked up to see George staring.

Presently he moistened his lips.

"What price the champagne?" he said softly.

And with his words every light in the place went out.

The tune the band was playing came to a discordant stop, and sounds of confusion arose upon every side. Tables were overturned and women cried out, and all the noise of a general hasty movement came to our ears. Here and there matches were struck, and the transient light they shed showed that everyone was for leaving with inconvenient speed. Men and women were scrambling from boxes into the promenade, and those in the promenade were climbing over the barrier on to the floor, and even the orchestra was feverishly deserting its pitch – all this, of course, to no purpose, for the exit was very small and, to judge from the cries and curses, was already pretty well blocked.

Such commotion seemed to me curious, for to stand or sit still until the lamps were relighted was common sense. Then it came to my mind that the regular patrons of the café were probably wiser than I and knew that *The Square of Carpet* was not the place to frequent when the lights had gone out.

And that was as far as I saw until I had made my way to the door of the box.

This was fast, and when I sought for the handle, there was none to be found.

For a moment I groped vainly: then the whole truth of the matter stood out clear as day.

Grieg's game had been very simple, but quite good enough for us.

He had waited for us to come home and let us hear where he was going that we might come too. He was known at *The Square of Carpet*, which was doubtless an infamous place and was clearly very well suited for the commission of crime. A stranger went there at his peril. Drugged wine and darkness to order were part of its stock-in-trade. We had, of course, been expected: we had been led to our box by a roundabout way, and the beer which we had ordered had been withheld.

When I told George that there was no handle, I heard him draw in his breath.

"Time to be going," he said. "Can we break down the door?"

That this was out of the question I very soon found. The door was stoutly built and opened inwards, and the back of the box itself was reinforced.

There was nothing to do but enter one of the boxes which stood on our right and left: this, of course, from the front, and, though such a movement was simple, the darkness made it a more unpleasant business than I ever would have believed.

We were now uncertain whether to use the passage or stay where we were, for our way by the passage was long and very narrow and those who were coming to seek us were probably on their way. To wait, however, seemed idle, for we were unarmed, and our only chance of avoiding a brush of some sort was to gain the exit before the crowd was gone.

We therefore opened the door and started along the passage as best we could, encountering no one, but quite unable to listen to any purpose for the uproar which filled the place.

Our progress was the most wretched I ever made.

We seemed to be stumbling forever round the wall of the bottomless pit. Grope as we would, we could not find the stairway up which we had come, and though more than once we entered boxes to try to get an idea of where we were, the darkness and the smoke and the noise were so confounding that Grieg himself could not have wished us more perplexed. Add to this that we were half stifled and were streaming with sweat, for now we were wearing our coats and the atmosphere of the passage was as thick and foul again as that of the box.

At last George touched my shoulder.

"I must drink or faint," said he. "My head's going round."

There was plainly no time to be lost.

George could endure like a lion. When he confessed that he was failing the end was at hand.

It occurred to me suddenly that, in the rush to be gone, all manner of liquor must have been left undrunk.

I groped for the door of a box, opened it and went in gingerly, feeling my way.

At once I touched the table and then, to my delight, a bottle heavy with wine.

George was close behind me, leaning on the jamb of the doorway with a hand to his head.

"Here's luck," said I quietly.

Then I put the bottle to his lips and helped him to drink.

"That's better," he said at last. "I'll be all right in a minute. Curse this heat."

I took the bottle from him to set it down, but I could not find the table and put out my other hand to act as a sounding-rod.

Almost at once it brushed something soft and, warm to the touch.

It was a girl's cheek.

I recoiled naturally. Then a dreadful suspicion leaped into my mind.

Desperately I strove to disprove it – only to prove it true.

The girl's head was down on the table, and she was sleeping like the dead.

The wine was our own wine, and the box was the one we had sat in ten minutes before.

5

The Vials of Wrath

If time had seemed precious but a moment ago, I had now set up the sand-glass in very truth.

George Hanbury's minutes were numbered. In a quarter of an hour, at most, he would be down and out, and how long he would be senseless heaven alone could tell.

When I told him what I had done, I heard him start. Then he threw back his head and began to laugh.

"You must admit it's funny," he said. "The vicious circle's nothing. We've looped the immoral loop. That's not so bad for a drug-fiend. I wonder how long I shall last."

But I could not laugh with him, and I think he only jested for my sake to keep up my heart.

How we had missed the stairs I could not conceive. They could not be hard of access, for everyone else on our level had been gone out of earshot before we were out of our box. Yet we had passed no staircase, nor so much as a gap in the wall.

Suddenly I saw that the stairs must lead out of a dummy box and that we must have gone clean past them, expecting and trying to find them upon the opposite side...

At once we decided to make a great effort to gain them before the drug took effect. This, of course, by entering every box until we came to the dummy that hid the head of the stairs.

I was now armed in some sort, for I had never put down the mischievous bottle of wine, and, though I longed for a pistol, I felt sorry for whoever might oppose me until the bottle was broke.

We entered the passage again, using what caution we could and listening carefully, for the hubbub below us was fainter and an echo answered such cries as still arose.

We had entered, I think, three boxes without result and were in the act of emerging to try the fourth when the flash of a light behind us betrayed a torch.

At once we shrank back, and when I had put the door to, I watched the light approaching by means of the crack I had left.

Its approach was slow and fitful. Now the beam was thrown forward to flood the passage with light, and now it was plainly directed into a box, for, when the passage was dark, I could see the play of its radiance upon the fronts of the boxes on the other side of the floor. Whoever was using the torch was making a thorough search.

Very soon I heard the footfalls of more than one man, and George, who was now armed as I was, touched my arm.

"Let them come in," he whispered, "and meet it on the back of the head."

I nodded my assent.

Three boxes away, however, the search came to an end.

"By —, they've gone!" screeched Grieg. "This is their — box. Go and fetch one of those swine from the head of the stairs."

Somebody blundered off the way they had come, and Grieg stood still waiting, with his torch pointing down at the ground.

So far as I could judge, the stairs were some ten boxes distant, for, after perhaps half a minute, I saw a fresh light approaching and heard the steps of two men.

Grieg hailed the newcomer fiercely.

"You've let them go by, you —. They're not up here."

"They must be," declared the other.

"I tell you they're not," raved Grieg. "I've been into every box."

His words amazed me, for I could have sworn them untrue. Yet why should Grieg be lying? Why...

Then in a flash I perceived the peculiar truth.

Our 'vicious circle' had saved us as nothing else could have done. Grieg must have entered our box very soon after we had left it by climbing into the next and, finding us gone, *immediately followed behind us*, searching the boxes as he went. And now he had gone full circle, as we had done, and, because he had not found us, believed us escaped.

"Every — box," Grieg repeated, stamping his foot.

I could hear the man protesting that we had not gone by the stairs.

"Then where are they gone?" barked Grieg. "Answer me that."

"They have not gone by," said the other, "since the lights were put out. With my torch I saw every being that used the stairs."

"I saw them myself in this box the instant before."

"Then are they here, Major." Instinctively he lowered his voice. "Perhaps – "

"I tell you I've been the round, and they're not on this floor. Is there any way out but the staircase?"

"There's a trap in the roof," said the other. "But how could they ever find that in darkness like this? I could not find it myself. It leads out of one of the boxes, but I cannot say which."

"Seventeen," murmured his companion.

"Is it shut?" said Grieg.

"It is always shut," said the other – a statement I fully believed.

There was a moment's silence.

Then –

"Very good," said Grieg, grimly. "It comes down to this. If they didn't go by you, the swine must be here."

"I have said so, Major."

"Not so fast," said Grieg. "It follows that, if they're *not* here, they must have gone through your hands." He paused significantly. "Now we're going to look once more – you and I together, my friend. I'll go round this way and you can go that, and if we don't find them between us – I go to Weber tomorrow at ten o'clock. But for me, he'd have closed this hell-hole two years ago."

With that, he bade the third man repair to the head of the stairs, and the fellow was off like a rabbit, as though he were glad to be gone.

The next moment the search had begun.

Here let me say that, though all these things have taken some time to tell, not more than five minutes had passed since Hanbury had drunk the drugged wine, and, as the two girls had survived for some fifteen minutes, I began to have hope that we might yet win safety before he collapsed. But George had, of course, drunk deep and had taken his portion at a draught.

Now, which way Grieg was going I could not tell, but I prayed that he was coming our, way; for he was sure to be armed, and if I could knock him senseless, his pistol, I was ready to wager, would bring us clear of the place.

With this heathenish prayer on my lips, I drew back into a corner beside the door, while George took his stand on the opposite side of the box.

From where I now stood, I could no longer see the light of our enemy's torch, and, what was disconcerting, I could not hear him approaching or any sound that he made.

Feverishly I strained my ears.

If they had changed their plan, and he was not coming, our course must be altered, too. If –

There, I think, my heart stood still. The fellow was at the next box – I could hear the movement of his clothing as he lifted an arm.

If he gave that sign of his presence he gave no more, and though the moments slid by he never moved. He seemed to have made up his mind to stay still where he was.

It occurred to me that he had heard us – was listening again, to make sure, before he gave the alarm. This was now possible, for the floor of the house was empty, and in place of the recent uproar, a horrid, deadly silence possessed the place. In the distance a glass shivered, and I guessed that his fellow was to blame. What remained of the drugged wine had already soaked my shirt-sleeve, and all my forearm was wet.

All these things I digested, but the man never moved. He might have known that time was his ally and that the longer he waited the nearer George came to collapse.

The box smelled very stale. Perfume, tobacco and liquor had done their work, and the sordid plush and hangings told an offensive tale. Yet people had sat there that night and would sit there the next and the next – unless Weber…

The man was moving.

As he entered the box I hit him full on the temple – an ugly blow. The bottle shivered, and the fellow reeled against George, who held him up.

I caught his torch as he dropped it, and together we laid him down.

I turned the beam on to his face. This was streaming with blood, but I knew it for the face of the man who had greeted us on our arrival and brought us upstairs…

I flashed the torch round the box for Grieg to see, and listened with all my might.

No sound came to my ears. The noise of the bottle breaking had meant nothing to Grieg.

"George," I whispered, "are you fit?"

"Yes," he breathed. "A – a little drowsy, you know."

"We'll do it yet," said I. "Box Seventeen."

I felt the man's pockets for a pistol, but he had no weapon upon him nor had one fallen from his hand.

The next box was numbered 'Twelve.'

Hoping very much that Grieg was not so sure of his bearings as to find suspicious the sudden advance of our torch, we hastened along the passage to 'Box Seventeen'. A glance at the filthy roof showed us the trap.

At the same instant, in the box directly opposed, we saw the flash of Grieg's torch. Any moment its beam might betray us, but in view of George's condition I dared not wait.

In an instant I had set the table beneath the trap, and, while George held the sorry block steady, I mounted and put up my hands.

I was able to touch the trap – with two inches to spare.

Now the trap was neither hinged nor fastened, but only sunk into place, and I had it free in a moment and ready to come away: but I dared not cast it outward for fear of the clatter it might make, so I disengaged it carefully and lifted it clear and down.

"Here, George," I whispered, and gave it into his hands.

He received it, certainly, but the wood was heavy, and I had asked too much of my failing friend.

Somehow he let it go, and it fell with a hollow clatter that could have been heard in the street.

"Oh, my God," he said faintly: and Grieg called out sharply and I saw the eye of his torch.

I was down on the floor with an arm about Hanbury's shoulders, holding him up.

"One more effort," I breathed. "On to the table, George, and I'll put you up."

I felt him brace himself. Then he mounted the table and put up his arms.

"Ready?" said I, taking hold, and felt him nod.

I thrust with all my might, and I am a powerful man.

He was up, out – waist-high out of the trap, when his body suddenly sagged.

The last effort had been too much, or – irony of ironies – the fresh air had abetted the drug.

"George!" I shouted. "George!"

I might have called upon the dead.

He hung there, between earth and heaven, with his arms spread without the building and me below, like Atlas, holding him up.

And after a little, finding his weight too heavy, I let him slide back slowly into my arms.

Then I laid him down on the floor, took off my overcoat and waited for Grieg.

I had now no weapon, for George had lost his bottle and there was none in the box: but my nerves were much more steady than they had been when I was waiting to fell Grieg's man. This may seem curious, for our plight was now more desperate than it had been before, but I have once or twice been at variance and have found the entrance to a quarrel more trying than the quarrel itself.

Had I had time I would have carried George Hanbury into another box, for Grieg must have seen our endeavour to escape, by the roof and, if he remembered the number, would make straight for 'Box Seventeen': but I dared not be caught in the passage with George in my arms and, as I dismissed the notion, I heard the murmur of voices five or six paces away.

Grieg was bringing the men from the head of the stairs.

I cannot think why I had failed to foresee so obvious a move. But at least I could read its lesson – that three men armed to one whose hands are empty are odds which no one can face.

In a flash I was out of the box and was wrenching at the handle of its door – the handle without, which a man must use to come in. Happily the metal was base, for almost at once it snapped. I whipped back into the box and slammed the door.

As I did so, three men came running...

I heard Grieg feel for the handle and let out a frightful curse. A moment later he flung his weight upon the door.

For this at least I was ready, for my back was braced against the opposite side, and so far from budging the woodwork, I think he but bruised himself, for he did not repeat his assault.

It now seemed clear that they would attempt to enter from one of the boxes which stood upon either side, but I did not envy them the venture and I do not think they liked it themselves, for they whispered a lot together before I saw the glow of a torch emerging from the box on the right.

I had turned to counter this manoeuvre in some confidence and was flat against the side of the box, awaiting the arm or the leg which must be thrown round the partition and over the balustrade when a deafening roar on my left told me that Grieg had fired directly into the lock of the door.

This, however, did not fly open, and the fellow flung himself against it with a passionate oath.

A kick would have done the business.

Beneath his weight, the door gave way, as though it had never been latched: not meeting the resistance he looked for, Grieg crashed into the box and, fouling the table, fell headlong on to the floor.

I was upon him in an instant, and, remembering that he was left-handed, had caught his left wrist, whilst with my other hand I took the man by the throat.

For a second, perhaps, he lay still. Then he struck me a blow on the temple that I can feel to this day. I thought my neck was broken, but, though I felt sick and dazed, I had the sense to hold on and to raise my elbow to parry his second blow. I felt his fingers seeking my throat, but I had the reach, and though his nails scratched me he could not take hold. Then he heaved like a horse that is down, and before I knew what was happening, the fellow was up on his knees, and so was I.

He had, of course, hoisted himself by the balustrade, but I think that movement will show the strength he had, for he had to lift both of us up, and I am a heavy man.

Again he sought my throat, but I shook him off. And that I think was a feint, for an instant later he gave another heave and brought us up to our feet. As we came up he turned and, before I could get my balance, I was back to the balustrade.

I now saw that he meant, if he could, to break my back, and that each of his three great efforts had been made to that end. Them I had not foreseen: but now, by the grace of God, I foresaw the fourth.

As he flung himself forward, I managed to writhe to one side, so that we both fell sideways on to the balustrade, and though he strove like a madman to roll me round, I was ready for this endeavour and brought it to nought.

By this time my strength was failing, and if one of the others had come to Grieg's assistance I must at once have succumbed: but Grieg could not call upon them because I was gripping his throat, and though, no doubt, they would have obeyed his orders, I fancy they were glad of an excuse for standing away from a pistol which might any moment go off. Yet, even without their aid, their leader was wearing me down.

It was only by the greatest endeavour that I could keep his pistol in check, and though I had a hold on his throat my fingers were aching unbearably under the strain.

He struck me again savagely and I shook him with all my might: he flung back into the box and dashed me against the wall: he tried to trip me and slammed me over the heart: then he put up his hand and tore my trembling fingers away from his throat.

I confess he deserved this triumph, for, though his lungs must have been bursting, he had made all the running and had never once ceased to attack.

I could hear him striving to shout, but his voice was gone. Then he sought my throat again, but I caught his wrist.

We were now both much exhausted and breathing hard, and only the thought of the pistol kept me from letting him go. Indeed, I was desperate, for I had the feeling that he was nursing his strength and that after a moment or two he would break away.

All at once I became aware that trouble of some sort was brewing without the box, for I heard a gasp of protest and the fall of a heavy body upon the stone; but before I could think what this meant, Grieg made a mighty effort to shake me off.

I am ready to confess that he did with me as he pleased, except that he could not free his pistol arm. I might have been a man of straw, so lightly did he fling and buffet me this way and that. I had to release his right wrist that my left hand might go to the help of my right, and so met a punishment that bade fair any moment to lay me low. Indeed, I hung on blindly, like a man in a trance.

Had he cared to drop the pistol I am sure that he could have killed me, for I should have let his wrist go without a thought: but we were both beyond tactics and even our instinct was failing beneath the strain.

Suddenly the box was illumined as bright as day.

The light came from behind me and fell on George Hanbury's face.

He was lying as I had laid him, and the table had fallen across him with its legs in the air. And that is why, I suppose; we had not trampled upon him, for whenever we touched the table we had, by one consent, contrived to sheer off for fear of becoming involved.

At this moment Grieg's wrist was up, but, he swept it down with a ghastly croak of triumph, and before I could grasp his meaning, fired full at George's face.

The horror of that action sent the blood to my head.

The fury of hatred possessed me as never before, and I think I was mad for a moment and was given a madman's strength.

He must have resisted my onslaught, but I cannot remember that he did so, and he might have been a lay figure for all the opposition I knew.

I tore the pistol from his fingers and hurled it down. Then I took him by the throat with both hands, thrust him to the front of the box and cast him bodily over the balustrade.

As I swung about, panting –

"Well done, sir," said Bell's voice.

The light of his torch blinded me, and I bade him throw the beam on to George and went down on my knees.

There was upon him no blood that I could see, but he, of course, was senseless and could not speak for himself. I therefore dragged off his coats and turned him about, but his shirt as far as his waist was nowhere stained. As I laid him back I noticed a graze on his chin which might have been made by a bullet that passed him by. Recalling as well as I could the angle at which the infamous shot had been fired, I ripped away the carpet at the edge of the box and there to my relief saw a bullet sunk in the wood.

"He missed him," I said unsteadily, and very near burst into tears.

Then I got to my feet and leaned back against the wall.

"Who have you got there?" I said.

"I don't know, sir," said Bell from the doorway. "There's one lying out in the passage, and this one put up his hands."

"Give me the torch," said I.

I saw a tall pock-marked fellow, with beady eyes, good enough, I should say, for a murder, but not very fond of a fight, for he looked the picture of terror, and, feeling my eyes upon him, he wrung out a sickly smile.

"D'you belong to this café?" I said.

He shook his head.

"Then why are you here?"

"I often come in the evenings."

"And sometimes you're wanted," said I, "for this sort of work."

He made me some shuffling answer I could not understand.

"Did you know the lights would go out?"

He nodded fearfully.

"Who told you?"

"The manager gave me a sign."

"What did you do then?"

"I went to the head of the stairs."

That was enough for me. The man was a common bully, known to *The Square of Carpet* and always ready for hire.

"Listen," said I. "We shall both of us know you again. If you lie about tonight's work you can pray for your soul."

The fellow grinned horribly and seemed to sag at the knees.

I told him to turn to his left and lead the way...

The manager was lying as we had laid him down, but his heart was beating strongly and the blood from the wound on his head was beginning to cake. By his side lay a loaded truncheon, caught by a thong to his wrist. I had missed it when I searched him, for his sleeve had fallen upon it when we laid the man down; and truly the sight of it shocked me, for I ought to have known that the man would never have sought us without a weapon of some kind, and had I but looked till I found it neither George nor I would have had so narrow an escape.

We returned to 'Box Seventeen'.

The man that Bell had knocked senseless was now showing signs of life, and, when he was fit to sit up, I drove him on to his feet. Then I bade him and his comrade take up George Hanbury gently and carry him down to the door. Bell went before them, and I, with Grieg's torch and pistol, followed behind.

We were down at last and were standing in the sinister hall.

There Bell and I took George Hanbury, holding him up between us, with his arms round our necks.

Then I addressed the two men.

93

"No doubt you'd like to clear out, but you won't do that. My friend was drugged. The manager went for me and I knocked him out. Major Grieg fired at my friend and I threw him out of the box. You're going to go to the police and tell them these facts. Excuse yourselves if you can: but tell half a lie about me and I'll hunt you down and break you as you deserve. And now lead on. If you try to escape we shall shoot. Make straight for the cathedral. Accost the first policeman you see and take no notice of us."

We passed out into the street.

There was a policeman on duty, pacing the cathedral square. At a nod from me the two walked boldly towards him, and, when I had seen them accost him, Bell and I bore away. A moment later we were beneath the shadow cast by the church.

We found a sheltered corner, and there I sat down, with Hanbury lying beside me and his head in my lap.

And, while Bell ran for the Rolls, I fell asleep.

If I slept then, I slept no more that night; but passed the hours in an infirmity of purpose of which I shall always be ashamed.

In the ordinary way I should have summoned a doctor, for I had no means of telling whether George was in danger or no. Yet, if there was trouble to come, my disclosure of George's condition would involve us up to the neck.

That trouble was coming seemed likely. That I had killed Grieg seemed certain, for he fell some sixteen feet and had uttered no sound. I found it hard to believe that, if he were dead, no action would be taken to bring his assailant to book.

Of the ultimate result of such action I had no fear, but I greatly feared an inquest at which I should be cross-questioned and requested to furnish a reason for Grieg's attempt upon our lives.

It follows that, unless one was needed, to call in a doctor was the last thing I wanted to do – yet, if Hanbury's condition required one, the very first.

Between these two courses I hovered, as a dog between two masters that are calling him different ways, with my hand upon George's pulse, which I was forever locating and immediately losing again.

I was so much occupied with my dilemma that not until Bell was leaving to go to his bed did I remember to ask him how he happened to be in the background at the moment when I needed him most.

His tale was soon told.

"I knew you weren't armed, sir, and all of a sudden I wondered if it might be a trap: so I put the Rolls away and walked back to see. Just as I got there people were coming away; but I didn't see you. When they were all of them gone, I went inside. It was all in darkness, and I was just turning away, when I heard something fall with a crash The next moment you called Mr Hanbury. Of course I knew from your voice there was something amiss, but I had no torch of my own, and I thought I should never reach you till I found the foot of the stairs."

"We owe you our lives," said I.

"Oh, no, sir," said Bell.

"Yes, we do. But for the light of your torch, Grieg wouldn't have seen Mr Hanbury and wouldn't have fired. It was that that made me see red and throw him out."

This was the plain truth: and I am very certain that, if Bell had not had the wit to go to *The Square of Carpet*, neither George nor I would have ever been seen again. Indeed, I learned later on that the place was believed to be the grave of several strangers who, finding nowhere to sleep, had gone to *The Square of Carpet* to make a night of it and had been, poor fellows, so cordially abetted in this artless enterprise that they had been seen no more.

It was past midday when to my great relief George Hanbury opened his eyes. What was more, beyond a shocking headache and an astonishing thirst, he seemed not one penny the worse and was all agog in an instant to hear my tale.

That trouble might come of Grieg's death he would not allow, "because," said he, "who goes to *The Square of Carpet* goes to the wars: enter that den of thieves and you put yourself out of court." Though I agreed that we had now little to fear – for the only witnesses of our concern with the matter would, I was sure, respect my menaces – I could not help thinking that Vigil could scarce be so lawless that no hue and cry would be raised: but the question was never settled, because, except in our mouths, it never arose.

Grieg's bodyservant was sent for that afternoon, and that evening our butler told Rowley that Grieg had had the misfortune to break both his legs. If his life was ever in danger I do not know, but, all things considered, I count him a fortunate man. I imagine he held his tongue – as did everyone else. What story was told to the police I neither know nor care, but I doubt that they asked any questions or did any more than bestow the injured men.

For myself, I was very stiff, and one side of my face was bruised and something swollen from temple to chin: but the following day the swelling had disappeared, and since my eye was not black, no one, I think, would have known that I had suffered violence of any sort. This was as well, for the day after that was Wednesday, and the butler had procured us two stalls for the gala performance of *Tosca* which the Grand Duchess was to attend. Still, I was well content to fleet two days securely, passing much of my time in the loggia and generally taking my ease, for our hour at *The Square of Carpet* had shaken me, and, whenever I see the word 'death-trap', I think of a row of boxes and a passage that has no end.

Though we rested, we did not waste time, but continually reviewed the position in the hope of perceiving some way of mating Johann.

George very soon came round to my way of thinking, namely, that command of the palace was as good as command of the throne; but, though we approached the pass from a hundred angles, we could see no feasible way of preventing or even of curing the mischief which the death of the Prince would most surely unloose.

Morning and afternoon the Grand Duchess drove out with Duke Paul. If the papers may be believed, their visits afforded great pleasure wherever they went. How much of that emotion was inspired by the sight of Duke Paul I cannot tell, but though the reports made good reading and though I was sure that Johann must bear the Grand Duchess a grudge, I could not believe that he had just cause for alarm and I could not see Riechtenburg rising to pull him out of the saddle and set up Duke Paul.

We never questioned Bell or Rowley about their new work, relying upon them to tell us if anything happened of which we ought to be told. On Tuesday they came back radiant, because they had driven Sully, who had, it seemed, talked to them freely and had shaken them both by the hand. "And, if you please, sir," said Rowley, "speaking of Maintenance, he said that the house was well named, and her ladyship laughed and cried out 'Like masters, like men.' " When I spoke of the morrow, they said the Grand Duchess had said that she would not need them by day, but that she would be glad of their service at half past eight that night.

I had expected so much and was considerably tempted to make one of the crowd at the doors of the opera-house, to give myself the pleasure of watching my lady arrive; for I was childishly eager to see her using our car as a state conveyance and our servants waiting upon her and discharging their elegant office as best they knew. But, if I had done so, I could not have been in my place in time to witness her entrance into the house, and to miss that would have been foolish, for the occasion was extraordinary and Duke Paul's and her reception was sure to signify matter which I should be able to read.

Accordingly, Hanbury and I were in our seats in good time, with our eyes and our ears wide open and very well pleased with our stalls, which gave us an excellent view of the royal box.

The theatre was not very large. Its less expensive parts were already full, the white linen clothing of the peasants contrasting strangely with their neighbours' attire. A constant stream was filling the rest of the house, and a better opportunity of observing the burghers of Vigil I cannot conceive.

The women were mostly handsome and very smart, but few wore jewels of any value, and I do not remember one vulgar or copious display. The men, though courtly, were not very well turned out: but they were a shrewd-looking lot, reserved, slow alike to laughter and wrath and not at all of the kind that is carried away. There were several officers present, all of them wearing full dress: quite a third of these were clad in the black and gold of the Black Hussars – a fact which mildly surprised me, for I had imagined that bodyguard duty permitted but little leave and that all the regiment was as good as confined to barracks until that duty was done.

This opinion was swiftly confirmed.

"Half the Body Guard's here," said a man who was seated behind me. "That comes of a colonel who has the ear of the Prince."

"It's irregular," said his companion, "But Johann is a law to himself."

"He fears the Prince," said the other.

"Soon he will have no one to fear," was the dark reply.

Here I missed a sentence or two, for George and I had to rise to allow some newcomers to pass.

As we sat down –

"He is not popular enough," said the man who had spoken first. "The people's darling can take his neighbour's wife, and the world will dance at his wedding: but anyone else will have to change his café."

98

"My friend," said the other, "I think you employ seven clerks. Because there are fireworks at the palace, are you going to give them a holiday that they may go and throw stones?"

I could not hear the answer, but I could guess what it was.

"A hundred years ago," said the other, "the throne touched every shepherd that sleeps on the hills: but now a penny stamp costs three half pence, no matter whose image it bears."

Here the orchestra began to tune up, and a rustle of expectation ran through the house. Everyone's face was turned to the royal box, and a little knot of people that had not taken their seats was held by an attendant in a doorway against its will.

I heard the conductor's baton strike on his music-stand.

Then the footlights went up, the music burst out and everyone got to their feet.

The Grand Duchess was in all her glory. A diamond tiara adorned her beautiful head, diamonds flashed from her throat and a heavy diamond bracelet was blazing upon her left arm. Over her white silk frock the crimson sash of some order hung from bare shoulder to waist.

As she came to her place, the cheering broke out, but, instead of bowing, she turned at once to Duke Paul who had followed her in. As he took his place, she made him a reverence – this very slowly and with infinite grace, and I am glad to say that he bowed low in return. Then they turned to the house and bowed their thanks, she making it very clear that the homage rendered was his and falling back a little to point her argument.

The Duke was in uniform and bore himself well enough.

In the midst of the scene, which was very cordial, a man stepped out of the background to stand between the Duke and my lady in the front of the box.

It was Duke Johann – come to share a triumph he could not prevent.

I saw the Grand Duchess observe him and I saw her start of surprise. The next instant her little gold bag fell into the aisle below.

As a voice cried 'Hurray for Johann,' she addressed Johann and pointed, and I saw him look down.

With her hand still pointing to the gangway, she smiled and spoke again and looked him full in the face.

The gesture was unmistakable. She was requesting him to send someone to recover her bag.

I never saw her look so charming, so gracious and so royal.

Johann was gravelled.

Obey, and he was her servant: refuse, and he was no gentleman.

For a moment the fellow wavered. Then he turned to the back of the box.

As the cheering died suddenly down, the Grand Duchess took her seat, and the Duke took his. An instant later the lights in the house were lowered, and the overture was begun.

"And so to bed," murmured George. "I'll bet a ducat that Johann has sent for his car. And I don't envy his chauffeur – or his ox or his ass or anything that is his. I've seen styles cramped before: but that was a permanent wave."

The first act was over, and we had just risen and passed to the end of our row, when a servant of the theatre was beside us and was asking very respectfully if we would show him the counterfoils of the tickets which had vouched for our seats.

When I produced mine, he immediately handed me a note upon which was written in pencil the number of my stall.

That this was from the Grand Duchess I had little doubt, for I had told Bell how to find me in case any need should arise.

The servant did not wait for an answer, but left at once.

I opened the note quickly.

Anger has been burned to the ground. May I have the car to drive there this very night?

I thrust the note into my pocket and turned to George.

"Come to the hall," I said.

George told me later that I was trembling with rage. I daresay it is true. For I knew that Anger had been burned, not by accident, but by design.

No matter whose hand had done it, Johann was the fountain of malice from which this horror had sprung.

The Grand Duchess was dangerous. The burning of Anger would distract her – draw her away from the scene. More. A woman of less precious metal *could not have appeared at the theatre*, with her ears singing from such a barbarous blow. Besides, maybe it would teach her to keep her hand out of the pie.

George read the note and caught his lip in his teeth.

"Poor lady," he said quietly. "That's a hell of a price to pay for backing a rotten horse."

"I shall go with her," I said. "In Rowley's place." He nodded. "But promise me this – that, until I get back, you'll never go out alone. Our score's more heavy than hers. St Martin, Barabbas, Grieg and the use of the Rolls. Johann's got it in for us red-hot."

"I'll hold the fort," said George. "But for heaven's sake don't be long. If the Prince dies while she's away – well, it'll be a walkover for Johann. And, in view of this 'frightfulness' – because that is what it is – he ought to have to put up a fight."

Be sure I agreed with him.

A girl's home lay in ashes: a blackened ruin smoked where an aged castle had lifted its lovely head. That a man who could approve, if not order, so harsh a wickedness should not only go unpunished but actually profit thereby was not to be borne.

I was powerless and a stranger. Unless he played into my hands, Duke Johann of Riechtenburg had no more to fear from me than from the trout that lay in the mountain streams. It was

101

as likely that he would play into my hands as that those mountain trout would rise at a rubber doll: yet, if he could have known how the deed would move me, I think he would have spared Anger – by no means for love of me, but because one does not sow the seed of sheer hatred, however barren the soil.

Rowley was standing by himself on the farther side of the street, and, as soon as he saw that I saw him, he led the way to the Rolls.

After a moment's reflection I bade them drive me back to the flat. There I gave them their orders and changed my clothes: as luck would have it, Rowley's peaked cap and greatcoat fitted me fairly well. Whilst I was changing, Bell put up a small bundle and a little hamper of food; then we went out to the car and I took the driver's seat.

I turned to Rowley, who was wearing my coat and hat.

"Wait for Mr Hanbury," I said, "at the door of the house. He will be looking for you. Never let him out of your sight until we return. And don't let her Highness see you as she comes out."

"Very good, sir," said Rowley.

I turned to Bell.

"Her Highness will ask you for my answer to the note which she sent. The answer is 'Yes'. Stand between her and me as much as you can. She is to think it is Rowley driving the car."

We took in fuel at a garage, and I drove to where the Rolls had been standing when I had come out of the house. And there I sat by myself for an hour and a half, with Bell patrolling a corner twenty-five paces away.

I think I shall remember that street, its depth and its breadth and its shadows, until I die. Its silence and emptiness faithfully reflected the inaction to which I was miserably condemned, than which I would have suffered more gladly the most gruelling toil. I could not sleep for thinking: and, when I would have thought to some purpose, my fancies raged together, as the heathen, and I imagined vain things. I have seldom found time so slow, so heavy-laden and so unprofitable, and when at length other cars began to arrive and Bell advised me to approach the opera-house, the fever of rage had left me and I was sick at heart.

Johann might play his cards badly, and the Grand Duchess play hers well: but, play she never so wisely, she could not win, for the cards themselves were against her and she had nothing to play.

Bell lifted his hand again, and the police made room for me to bring the car to the steps…

All was now bustle and excitement.

So far as the traffic was concerned, the police maintained no order, and cars were approaching the building from every side. As may be believed, the confusion was very soon shocking, but at last, to my great relief, I saw a way being cleared for the royal car. This at a cost of convenience which I cannot compute, for the vehicles were massed together, and, if one was to move, then twenty or more must first move to give it place. To make matters worse, the police essayed at this juncture to take control, but, since they did not act in concert, they only aggravated the disorder which had to be seen to be believed. Indeed, I heard later that many of the audience walked home and that others awaited their cars for more than two hours.

When I first arrived, the steps were alive with officials, but no one else: almost at once, however, a crowd began to collect, and within a few moments people were standing ten deep to see the Grand Duchess go by.

I dared not look, but I saw the press sway and scramble and Bell's hand go up to his hat.

As I uncovered –

"Where's Johann?" cried a voice.

"Gone to his kennel," laughed someone, and the cheering broke out.

"Leonie! Leonie!" bawled the crowd, and one or two shouted "Paul!"

The goodwill towards the Grand Duchess was manifest, but, had he appeared without her, I think the Duke's welcome would have been very cold. Indeed, as they entered the car –

"Every couple's not a pair," said a man two paces away.

The door was slammed, and Bell took his seat by my side. As I let in the clutch –

"Leonie!" roared the crowd. "Leonie!"

And somebody cried "When's the wedding?" and two or three women "Sleep well."

When we were clear of the cars, Bell told me which way to take, and five minutes later we came to the fine, old mansion in which the Duke was lodged.

As we stopped, the house door was opened, and I saw the servants within…

The Grand Duchess was speaking in English…

"Please say 'Good night' and go."

"I'm damned if I will," said the Duke. "You've had your show and this is where I come in. Why shouldn't you sup with me?"

"Think it over," said the Grand Duchess.

"But, damn it, we're engaged," snarled the Duke.

"What of that?"

"Oh, don't be so sticky," said the Duke. "I'm sick of this play-acting business. Let's be ourselves."

"I'm not play-acting," said the girl. "I never play-act with you except on parade."

"Oh, put it away," said the Duke. "As my fiancée you get a hell of a show. If I liked, I could get in your way. But I don't – I let you have it. Look at tonight. Well, now it's my turn. I've a right to ask you to supper – "

"And I've a right to refuse. Please say 'Good night' and go."

"Not so fast," said the Duke.

"I'm tired," said the Grand Duchess.

I heard the Duke suck in his breath.

"If I were you," he said, "I should mind your step. I know you've a supper-party, and I know who's going to be there."

He got to his feet and descended heavily.

Then he addressed himself to Bell.

"You can tell your employers that her Highness has no further use for their car."

"Paul," said the Grand Duchess quickly.

I heard the fellow turn.

"Don't be foolish, Paul. We can't sup together alone, as you very well know. And, indeed, I haven't a party. You can come, if you like, and see."

There was a little silence.

The Grand Duchess had risen and was standing behind me by the open door of the Rolls.

"Why couldn't they lend *me* the car?" said the Duke sullenly.

"Well, you weren't very civil, Paul. I know you were very worried, but – "

"I don't know what the hell they expect – I'm not their class. Any way I'm getting tired. Fed up, Leonie. I'm sick of the sight of the house and I'm sick of parades. You have the — car, you have the show – I let you, and – "

"If you're patient, it'll soon be your show. I won't interfere – then."

"Good night," said the Duke suddenly.

She gave him her fingers to kiss, and he jerked her out of the car and into his arms.

I heard him kiss her soundly, but she made no noise.

Suddenly she was back in the Rolls, and its door was shut.

As the car slid forward, I heard the Duke's horse laughter offending the night.

With Bell for guide, I drove at once to the house at which Hanbury and I had dined three nights before.

As the Grand Duchess alighted –

"My note," she said tremulously. "What is the reply to my note?"

"The answer is 'Yes', my lady," said Bell.

I heard her stifle a sob.

"It is far," she said. "How – how soon will you be ready to leave?"

"We are ready now, my lady."

She did not speak again, but turned to the steps, and I heard a door opened and the voice of Madame Dresden begin to utter a greeting and come to a sudden stop.

When I ventured to turn my head, the Countess' arms were about her, and she was weeping like a child.

For the next thirty minutes I sat as though turned to stone, and Bell, beside me on the pavement, never once moved.

I do not wish to labour the matter or to give the Duke's behaviour a colour it does not deserve. As her affianced husband, the man had a right to demand that, when they met or parted, the Grand Duchess should give him her lips. I think he was afraid to do so. Be that as it may, he did not. Had he asked and she objected, vile as he was, he could not, I think, have been blamed for insisting upon his right. But he did not ask. He preferred to commit a vulgar, common assault upon the peerless creature who was fighting to save his throne. And there I will leave the business, for even at this distance of time I cannot recall it with composure and, indeed, I think her tears and his laughter are commentary enough.

So I sat, still as an image, staring through the windscreen, with the sweat drying salt upon my face.

Johann and his works I had forgotten. I could only remember the shortcomings of Duke Paul. When I asked myself why the Grand Duchess was striving in his behalf, I felt as though I were dreaming some monstrous dream.

At last a maid came with a dressing-case, and a moment later the Grand Duchess entered the car.

The night was clear and cool, the ways were empty and the mountain air refreshed both body and soul. Once clear of Vigil, we went like the wind and in less than forty minutes we had come to the frontier bridge.

Bell showed a pass to the sentries, arms were presented and we rolled on to Austrian soil.

Five minutes later –

"Stop, please," said the Grand Duchess. "I wish to sit in front."

In silence the change was made, while I furtively hunched my shoulders and sunk my chin on my chest.

We had covered a mile in silence before the Grand Duchess spoke.

"Thank you for coming," she said.

6

The Orchard at Littai

Drive as I would, the dawn was at Anger before us, and the sun was touching the mountains as we entered the three-mile gorge at the head of which the castle had stood.

We had made the journey in silence, and the Grand Duchess sat so still that more than once I thought that she was asleep: but, if ever I turned to make sure, I found that her eyes were open, and these would greet my movement to show that she was awake.

The gorge made a lovely passage at any hour, but at break of day it was, I suppose, at its best, and I shall ever remember how sweet the foliage smelled and how grateful was the sound of the torrent by which we sped. Movement through air so cool was most refreshing, and when I uncovered my head to make the most of it, I noticed that the Grand Duchess had done the same.

If she was weary, she showed no sign of it: if she was apprehensive, none would have guessed the truth. Her great grey eyes were steady, her head was high, and a quiet, resolute look sat on her face. I cannot compare her beauty, for I have not the words, but I think that a poet would have sung of the wind in her blue-black hair and the quiver of her delicate nostrils and the curve of her exquisite mouth.

I had passed through the gorge four times, and I knew my way. There was a beechwood that marked the end of it and masked the natural circus from such as came up by the water, much as a screen in a theatre may mask the wings. Once a man rounded this wood, circus, meadows and castle lay full in his view, but, until he did so, there was nothing to indicate that the gorge did not run before him for another three miles.

When we came to the beechwood I brought the Rolls to rest. As I stepped into the road –

"Will you wait here," I said, "until I come back?"

Before I had finished the Grand Duchess was out of the car.

"No," she said quietly. "If it were Maintenance – "

"I wish to God it were," I said warmly, and meant what I said.

My fervour brought a smile to her lips, of which I was very glad.

"I will go on," she said gently. "Follow me in five minutes, if you like: but not before."

With that, she was gone down the road, and a moment later the beechwood hid her from view.

I threw off my coats, made my way to the torrent and bathed my head and hands in a lively pool. Bell had a towel ready and, ere the five minutes were past, I had made a rude enough toilet, but one that refreshed my senses and did my heart good. Then I bade Bell be ready to serve what breakfast he could in half an hour and left him sponging the windscreen which was littered with insect dead.

I have several times seen the waste which fire has committed and twice the horrid ruin it has made of a country house: but the havoc wrought at Anger was of another kind. I had read of the ravages of earthquakes and wars and storms, but I had never so much as conceived a destruction so absolute by any element and I cannot believe that Carthage was ever so blotted out.

Not a wall was standing more than ten feet from the ground, and the island which the castle had occupied was now a black mound of refuse, walled for the most part, like a dunghill, and smoking leisurely. At one point a wall had fallen outwards, and a mass of stones and rubble was damming the stream; and the trees around were horribly disfigured, for such as had not been burned had had their foliage scorched, and the broad belt of dead black branches and shrivelled leaves stood out very sharp and ugly against the living green.

For the rest, next to nothing was changed.

The water ran as clear and as stoutly, and a gay cascade was seething over the new-made dam: except for a black spot or so, the sward was as fresh and as blowing as when I had seen it before; and the bridge held up by leopards was there to usher who would venture to the ghastly holocaust that had been the Grand Duchess' home.

At the verge of the meadows stood two ponies, fastened to pegs in the ground, and two oxen were couched beside them, regarding the world about them with comfortable eyes. By these my lady was standing, listening to the speech of a man who was clad as a groom, and surveying the desolation, with a hand to her throat.

I made my way over the turf to where she stood.

As I came up, she turned.

"The servants escaped, and the horses. Mercifully my great-aunt was not there. Karl says that petrol was pumped right over the battlements – literally pumped, through a hose. One of the drums they used is still in the bed of the stream. But they fired the stables first, and by the time he and Jacob had got the horses away whoever did it was gone. Jameson, the English butler, got out the maids. In less than two hours from the outbreak, it was as you see it now. Of course it was full of oak and there were beams in the walls. He says it was an absolute furnace: if it hadn't begun to rain while the fire was raging, he thinks the woods would be black for half a mile."

It was easy to picture the scene.

Six servants asleep in the castle, and only three of these men: the roar of the great waterfall, and the ceaseless fret of the torrent to smother irregular sounds: a malefactor up on the ramparts, which the trees overhung, and petrol pouring into the gallery and making its way down the stairs...

"Where are the horses?" I said.

"They are at Littai, a village four miles away. The servants are with them, and Karl will join them today. Perhaps you will take me there presently – now, if you're not too tired. I mean, I've seen what I came to see, and it's – well, it's no good my staying here."

The half-laugh, half-sob with which she said this would have bruised the hardest heart, and for the life of me I could not answer, but only nodded my head.

We passed across the meadows without a word.

As we came to the beechwood, she turned, to stand very still. And I stood still behind her, with my eyes on the ground.

I do not know how I knew it, but, as though she had told me, I knew that she was looking on the circus for the very last time and that, once she had rounded the beechwood, she would never come back...

Two minutes later we came into view of the car.

"Will you breakfast first?" I asked her. "I'm afraid we have nothing hot, but – "

"I am only thirsty," she said. "And, if you will wait, I will bathe my face and hands."

I carried her case to the water and set a cushion on the edge of the little pool. Then I sent Bell off in the Rolls, to turn her about, and mixed some brandy and soda against my lady's return.

This she was loth to drink, but, after a little entreaty, she did as I asked.

I put on Rowley's greatcoat and picked up his cap.

"Don't wear those things," she said quietly.

I hesitated, cap in hand.

"I think perhaps it's better," I said.

"I will not have you wear them," she cried, stamping her foot.

I gave the garments to Bell and entered the car.

There was at Littai a farm which the Grand Duchess owned, and, though it was tenanted, the farmer was her faithful servant and glad to offer his mistress the best that he had. Her hunters stood deep in his straw and ate his corn, her servants fed at his table and lay beneath his roof. A pleasant parlour had been set aside for her coming, and Jameson had appeared in the doorway as we drove up. The place might have been her home. But it was not. Leonie, Grand Duchess of Riechtenburg, was homeless. Anger had not been insured, and there was not left of it one stone upon another.

And there I will leave the business, for there, in that humble homestead, she left it herself.

"Anger is dead," she said quietly, within the hour. "Six hundred years ago they cut down the woods to build it, and now the woods will return and take it back. Nature is very forgiving. Nobody else would tend his enemy's grave... And now I'm going to try and put it out of my mind. It's rather like losing a dog – an old, faithful fellow that was so – so glad to see you whenever you'd been away." Her voice had begun to tremble, but she shook the tears from her eyes and started up. "This is the way of folly. I will not speak of it again."

Nor did she, that I know of. But her voice was big with weeping, and I left her to take her rest with a heavy heart.

At five of that afternoon I was sitting in the farmer's orchard with a pipe in my mouth.

The long grass was cool and fragrant, an aged apple-tree made me a rest for my back, and the murmur of bees about their business and the trickle of a neighbouring rill would have had me asleep in an instant, but for the rest I had taken an hour before.

Compared with these simple conditions, might, majesty and dominion seemed to me treacherous stuff, and God knows to what flights of philosophy I might not have soared, but I heard a rustle behind me and, before I could move, the Grand Duchess sat down by my side.

"I have been very obedient," she said. "I slept until half past three."

"I am very glad," said I.

"I think you are a good doctor," she said. "My nerve has come back."

"You never lost it," said I.

I saw her fine chin go up.

"I am not given to tears," she said coldly.

"You have the greatest heart that I have ever known."

"Because I don't know when I'm beaten? Never mind. How did you bring Grieg down?"

"He tried to kill Hanbury," I said. "And I threw him out of a box."

She knitted her brows.

"A box?"

"At *The Square of Carpet*."

Slowly she turned, to look me full in the eyes.

"How did you come to be there?"

"Grieg set a trap," said I. "And Hanbury and I walked in."

"And you swore that you would be careful. You – "

"It was a trap," I protested. "I never dreamed – "

"You are down enough upon others who break their word."

"I took every care," I said. "For one thing I had no idea that *The Square of Carpet* was the kind of place that it is. And Hanbury will tell you that – "

"Tell me yourself what happened."

Shortly I related our adventure, while she sat looking into the sunlit distance, with her knees drawn up a little and her delicate fingers laced about her slim legs.

When I had finished –

"You must leave Vigil," she said. "You are not safe there. Grieg was an instrument, but Johann's the power behind. And this morning you saw what he does to people who get in his way."

"I think *The Square of Carpet* was Grieg's own show."

"Directly, perhaps. But you've twisted Johann's tail."

"I'm going to," said I violently. "He'll curse the day he burned Anger before I'm through."

Her head was round in an instant and a finger up to her lip.

"That's not like you," she said. "When you talk like that you scare me. What have you got in your mind?"

"Nothing," I cried bitterly. "And there's the rub. I'm brainless, powerless, useless. And that's why I'm safe."

"But you said – "

"I know, I know. I can't help it. You see, he's burned down your home."

I had spoken without thinking. But, if that is a fault, it is not always a misfortune, and I cannot forget the light that my childish avowal brought into her glorious eyes or the exquisite smile that came to rest on her mouth.

"You are very downright," she said, looking away. "And you have been – very kind."

"You know I have not." I cried. "You know – "

"I know I am very grateful," she said gently, "and – " I heard her catch her breath " – and very honoured."

I got to my feet somehow and stepped to the brink of the brook. It was, I know, ungallant, but I could not sit still beside her, for the blood was surging in my temples and the flame of her charm and beauty had entered into my soul. I stood for a moment, watching the flow of the water and gripping the stem of a sapling till the bark broke under my hand. Then a great fear came upon me that she would go, and I turned and went back to where she sat in the grass.

"I won't leave Vigil," I said.

She looked up quickly.

"Once you said you would do whatever I asked."

"Then do not ask me to go – Leonie."

She put a hand to her head.

"Don't make it more hard for me," she said. "I came to you here in this orchard to send you away, to make you promise that tomorrow you would leave Vigil – and not come back. You say you're useless. Just think of what you've done… Time after time you've ridden Johann off. Take only our presence here. I *had* to visit Anger – *ça va sans dire*. If you hadn't brought me, I must have gone by train. From Vigil to Anger by train takes the whole of one day, I should have been out of Vigil not for one day, but for three – *as Johann meant me to be*. As it is, tomorrow morning I shall be back in my seat. Well, that won't amuse Johann… Grieg probably said he'd fix you, and Johann believed he would: now Grieg's on his back, and you're going as strong as before."

"What can he do?" said I.

"Make certain of you," she cried, clapping her hands to her eyes. "Blot you out – as Grieg nearly did. Your Minister will make inquiries, but what of that? England won't go to war because you are – not to be found. You've seen that the man is ruthless, and that is why you must go. If anything happened to you…"

"Answer me one thing," said I. "Is this the only reason why you wish me to go?"

She drooped her head and nodded.

"Will you swear that, Leonie?"

"Yes" – in a very low voice.

"I will not go," I said quietly.

Then –

"But I will disappear."

For a moment she stared at me. Then I saw understanding lighten her eyes.

"You mean?"

"I will disappear," said I. "So will George Hanbury. I don't know why I didn't think of it before. It was the obvious line."

"And the servants?"

"Will enter your service. To touch your chauffeurs is more than Johann will dare."

"When you say 'disappear' – "

"We shall appear to have gone. Our rooms will be empty, our luggage will in fact have gone. Witnesses will declare that we took the Salzburg express. They will be perfectly right. We shall take it openly, and Vigil will see us no more. Only the servants will know better: they will always be able to find us within the hour."

The Grand Duchess looked at the heaven with shining eyes.

"You are very skilful," she murmured. "It seems I am to have it both ways. Will you disappear tomorrow?"

"Yes, Leonie."

With a sudden movement she put up her little hands.

"I am very happy," she said, "to think that you will not be gone."

I lifted her to her feet, and she slid an arm through mine and led me down to the brook.

"I watched you," she said, "just now. I saw you look into the water. What did you see?"

"I saw your face, Leonie."

Her arm slipped away, and the colour came into her cheeks. With her eyes on the water, she spoke.

"Paul's accession means everything to me."

"I know that," I said. "I will try to bring it about."

She looked up quickly at that.

"Is it your way to be faithful to a dream?"

"I do not know," I said slowly. "I have not dug so deep. It is my great pleasure to help you – to what you want."

She drew in her breath a little, as though she would speak. Then she seemed to change her mind.

"I am sorry," she said at length. "Today it is I who am tongue-tied. I have nothing to say." She pushed back her hair from her temples. "Before we go back, will you drive me to a valley I know?"

"Yes."

"There is an old house there, standing on the Anger estate. It was built for a hunting lodge. It's in a bad way, I'm afraid: but they may be able to patch it, and you see I must have somewhere – I don't care how rough it is, but I must have a lodging of some sort to which I can always go."

"I'm half a mason," said I, "and I've seen worse joiners than George. We'll set it to rights with pleasure, when – when Johann has lost his match."

There was a little silence. Then –

"Tell me something you cannot do," she said.

I took her hand and put it up to my lips.

"There is nothing I cannot do for you," I said unsteadily. "I have never seen anyone like you in all my life."

Her cool fingers closed upon mine, and I think it was that movement that sent the blood to my head.

What I said I do not remember, but I know that I begged her to let me take her forever out of the intrigue and violence which seemed to be her portion and away from the dreadful future which threatened her lovely life.

I am no maker of speeches, but a schoolboy must have been eloquent with such a theme. It was not my cause I was pleading so much as hers, and of my love I said little, except that I would worship her always and that she would be my great lady although she bore my name.

She heard me out in silence, with my hand held tight between hers and her eyes on the distant hills. And when I had done, she still stood, like some precious statue, but a little paler than usual and very grave.

The gate of the orchard creaked, and I loosed her hand.

Then Bell came down through the grass, with a telegram on a tray.

The Grand Duchess opened it slowly. When she had read it through, she gave it to me.

Grand Duchess Leonie Littai
  Return

                                            Marya.

"There's no answer," she said quietly, and Bell withdrew.

"This can mean but one thing," she said. "Can we leave in a quarter of an hour?"

"Yes," said I.

We turned away from the water and made our way to the gate.

As I held it open –

"I'm sorry I forgot myself," I said.

I shall see the smile she gave me so long as I live.

"Oh, my dear," she cried, "I'm so glad you did."

We stopped at Bariche for petrol and reached the frontier just before ten o'clock.

We passed the Austrian sentries, and I drove the car over the bridge. When the Riechtenburg sentries opposed us, I beckoned and held out my pass, but, instead of moving to inspect it, they stood their ground, and one of them raised his voice and called the guard.

"It is her Highness," I cried, and Bell alighted and took the pass out of my hand.

The guard came tumbling out, and Bell went up to the sergeant and showed the pass, but the latter shrugged his shoulders and pointed to the front of the car.

Here an officer appeared, hastily adjusting his chin-strap, paper in hand.

As he came alongside, the Grand Duchess lifted her voice.

"I am the Grand Duchess Leonie. What does this mean?"

The officer saluted elaborately, and the sergeant called the guard to attention; but the sentries stood where they were.

"Your Highness will forgive me," said the officer, "but I have had definite orders not to admit this car."

The Grand Duchess put out her hand.

"Let me see them."

The officer saluted stiffly. Then he gave her his paper and saluted again.

It was a telegram.

Commanders of Frontier Posts
  Rolls-Royce bearing number-plates AM 7789 and GB in no circumstances and no matter how exalted its occupant is this car to enter Riechtenburg

Fensyl.

"Who is Fensyl?" said my lady.

"Your Highness, that is the War Office department under whose orders we lie."

"I will telephone," said the Grand Duchess. "Please get me through."

"I am desolated to inform your Highness that our telephone has not been working since five o'clock."

The Grand Duchess sat very still.

"I have been summoned," she said, "and I cannot wait. I will indemnify you." She handed the telegram back. "Give me a sheet of paper and I will write you an order that overrules that."

The other's eyes bulged from his head.

"Madam, I d-dare not," he stammered. "Your Highness will see from the order that it is specially framed to cover a – a possibility such as this."

"You know who I am, and I tell you that I am in haste. Do you take the responsibility of stopping me?"

The unfortunate man's face was shining with sweat.

"Madam," he cried, "I am not stopping your Highness. Had I been so ordered, I would have resigned my command. It is only the car, madam. Your Highness is as free as – "

"How can I walk? It is eight miles from here to Lesson where I may or may not get a car. And your telephone is not working."

"Madam, I am desolated, but I dare not let this car pass."

There was a little silence.

I leaned towards the Grand Duchess and lowered my head.

"Shall I risk it?" I murmured. "For fear of hitting you, they'll never dare shoot."

I saw her measure the distance between a sentry and me.

Then –

"No," she said.

Maybe she was right. The man had his bayonet fixed, and the car would have had to go slowly before it went fast.

"Shall I back," said I, "to the other side of the bridge? Then I'll put out the headlights and let her rip. They wouldn't expect her back, and – "

"No," said the Grand Duchess. "Nobody must be hurt. If you ran down a sentry, not even the Prince could save you from summary trial." She turned to the officer. "You will report this matter, and so shall I. In detail, please."

"Without fail, your Highness."

"I shall have pleasure in saying that you did your unpleasant duty with resolution and tact, and, when I am no longer Grand Duchess, I shall make it my business to remember your name."

The officer's relief and delight were pitiful to see, and his voice trembled with feeling as he strove to avow a devotion which plainly spoke for itself.

The Grand Duchess smiled and nodded and turned to me.

"We must go back to Bariche," she said. "Will you back the car?"

As I did so, Bell stepped aboard and the officer shouted an order and then saluted himself, standing with his hand to his helmet until we could see him no more.

So soon as we were clear of the frontier I brought the car to rest by the side of the road.

"We must try the next post," said I, and picked up the map.

The Grand Duchess looked at me curiously: but, when I looked inquiringly back, she averted her eyes.

"To be stopped again," she murmured.

"Not at all," said I. "Now we know what to expect."

She laid a hand on my arm.

"My dear," she said, "don't you see that this is a trap?"

"A trap?" said I.

"A trap. This is Johann's doing – we both know that. He seeks to delay my return: but he knows that you are with me and he knows that the man that broke Grieg is not afraid of knocking a sentry down. And so he invites you to do it – in my behalf." She drew in her breath. "You'd be arrested tomorrow and you'd lie in prison for years."

For a moment I thought very fast. Then I returned to the map.

"The next post is by Cromlec," I said. "Do you know that way?"

"Yes. It is in the mountains. There is no post upon the frontier itself. The Austrian guards are at Cromlec, a mile or so from the pass, and ours are at Vogue upon the opposite side."

"What could be better?" said I. "When we come to the top of the pass we simply switch off the engine and put out the lights. With any luck we shall not be so much as heard."

The Grand Duchess gazed through the windscreen, as though she had not heard what I said.

At length –

"It sounds very easy," she said. "But I cannot remember Vogue, and in any event I have never been by there by night. I think the road will be lighted – in front of the guard-room, I mean."

"We will stop before we come to the village, and I will walk on to see."

Again she hesitated. Then she turned and looked at me.

"Very well," she said.

Together we studied the map, to make sure of our way. The next minute we were heading for Cromlec as fast as we could.

It was about an hour later that we came to the top of the pass.

The night was lovely, but happily, very dark, and the air was cool but gentle, for all the winds were still.

The Austrian guards had not so much as stopped us, and, though I slowed down for their guard-room, a sentry who was eating an apple did nothing but nod his head. I call him a sentry because he was by the guard-room and was not asleep, but he had no rifle and was not wearing his tunic and he had the air of a man who is off duty and does not propose to be disturbed. This, no doubt, was because we were leaving his country, but such laxity gave me some hope that the watch which was kept at Vogue would be none too strict.

Thereafter, we had seen no one, and the liquid sound of a cow-bell, which now and then sweetened the night, was the only evidence that we had not the world to ourselves.

So, as I have said, we came to the top of the pass.

I brought the car to a standstill and put out her lights.

Now I dared not drive on until my eyes were something used to the darkness, for our headlights were very brilliant and had turned the night into day. I therefore left the car, to walk to the nearest bend and see, so far as I could, the course of the road beyond it and whether there were any places that called for particular care.

The Grand Duchess would have come with me, but I begged her to stay where she was and promised to return in a moment when I had seen what I could.

The petty reconnaissance proved extremely rich.

Hardly had I rounded the bend when the road became a mere shelf cut out of the mountainside. The brink was unfenced, and, when I had drawn very close, I saw, far away beneath me, a definite splash of light. This, of course, was coming from Vogue, or to make no bones about it, from the guard-room which we must pass: and I must confess that this danger signal shook me, for it seemed to me to argue an uncommon vigilance, and though I tried to remember that by night the flame of a candle may be seen a great way off, the light below me was by no means one point of radiance, but rather a flood of light shed, I was sure, by some lamp which I could not see.

After a little, I picked up the line of the road.

This descended by zigzags into the valley below and promised an easy passage, dark though it was; for its course had been ordered by man and not by Nature, and so should present no feature which a cool head might not expect.

Very thankful that I had happened to stop the Rolls where I had – for, had we rounded the corner and shown our lights, anyone looking from Vogue must surely have noticed their glare – I made my way back to my lady and told her that all was well.

A moment later we had started to steal down the pass.

Now the brink was upon my right hand, but the Grand Duchess sat on my left, and, since I gave the depths as wide a berth as I could, not until we had rounded a bend was she afforded a view of the light below.

When she saw it she caught her breath.

"It's hopeless," she cried. "Hopeless. Look at that light."

"I'm going to," I said quietly. "But not from here. I shall stop the car this side of the last of the bends. And then we'll walk on together and see what it means."

"You are very – imperative," she murmured.

The rebuke brought me to my senses, and I set my foot upon the brake.

"I beg your pardon," I said, "with all my heart. I should have told you my plan. You know that I did not mean it – but I am used to working with Hanbury, and he and I do each as the other says."

"I am in your hands," she said slowly. "You – you think that we should go on."

"My dear, what else can we do? If this little post is lively, the others will be broad awake. I have thought of the train, but God knows when there will be one, and Bell and I have left our passports behind."

"I am in your hands," she repeated. "Do as you will."

I let the car go forward…

Our passage was very slow, for I dared not show any light that was fixed to the car, and as luck would have it, neither Bell nor I had a torch; and though I had often driven without any lights and met with no accident, that was always upon a road that I knew and never upon one so perilous, upon which the slightest error would cost so dear.

At last, however, we were down, and though I could not be certain which was the last of the bends, I judged us to be near enough and brought the car to rest by the side of the road.

I bade Bell stay where he was and handed my lady out.

One thing I marked in our favour.

Somewhere, not far below us, there was a waterfall. No ordinary sound that we made could rise above its dull roar: if we were careful, therefore, we had nothing to fear but the light, unless, of course, a sentry were posted in the midst of the road.

The next bend was the last of the zigzag, but when we had rounded this, we still could not see the guard-room, for the road now followed some water, and after two hundred yards curled sharp to the right. It was when we had made this corner that we saw the style of the gauntlet we had to run.

Fifty yards away stood the guard-room, on the left of the way. It was built with a long porch or loggia fronting the road, to which three steps descended in a line with the guard-room door. From the roof of the loggia was hanging a powerful electric lamp whose light a reflector was throwing full on to the road. *And in the road stood a trestle, some ten feet long, with a lantern standing upon it and showing red…*

This side of the guard-room was a bridge, beneath which went roaring the water which we had heard, and the road was falling sharply the whole of the way. Nature was dead in our favour. We could have started the engine, attained a high speed *and been gone* before any sentry had time to turn his head – but for the barrier standing in the midst of the road.

I touched the Grand Duchess' arm.

"Will you go and get Bell?" I said. "Bring the Rolls down to this corner and wait for me?"

"What are you going to do?"

"See if there's a sentry," I said.

"Promise me you will do no violence of any kind."

"I promise," I said.

The next moment she was gone.

Now, though I had not said so, I had a high hope that the trestle was there to serve a lazy guard.

The post was plainly too petty to warrant an officer's presence, and day after day the guard could have little to do but while away the time. Such things do not make for discipline… I would have laid a small fortune that they were all asleep.

I should have lost my stake.

The sentry was standing in the porch on the farther side of the light.

His back was towards me, and he was leaning on the loggia's wall – which was, upon the inside, waist high – gazing down the valley which led to the Vigil road. His rifle stood up beside him against the wall. The door of the guard-room was open, and all was dark within.

Standing there, in the shadows, I could not think what to do.

The trestle, the sentry and the powerful electric light were working together for evil, and working extremely well. Any two of the three I could, I think, have eluded without any fuss: but the three together were presenting an obstacle which I could not see how to approach, much less surmount.

125

The trestle had to be moved. It did not look very heavy, and I had no doubt that I could put it aside without any noise: but the road where the trestle was standing was as bright as though it were lighted by the midday sun.

I had promised to use no violence: I must therefore suffer the sentry and *any armed interference* the fellow might make. This was serious. With the Grand Duchess in my charge, I dared take no such risk.

I must not meddle with the sentry, and, lest the sentry should turn, the trestle I dared not touch. Only the light remained.

I slunk as close as I dared. Then I lifted my head to look over the loggia's wall.

By the side of the guard-room door was a dirty switch. From this ran a flexible cord, loosely stapled to the wall and rising to the roof of the loggia, where I could see it no more. That switch and wire were serving the powerful lamp no one could have doubted for an instant. The thing was patent as the nose upon a man's face.

At once I saw the value of darkness – of sudden, blinding darkness to our attempt.

If that powerful lamp were to fail – fail suddenly, silently and for no obvious reason, *as is the common way of electric lamps*, not only would the sentry be embarrassed, but, what was far more important, his attention would be so much distracted that a caravan of cars could steal by and he know no more of their passing than the peasants asleep in their beds.

Now I cannot foresee, as can some, the action which, faced with certain conditions, another will take. I have always coveted such foresight as being a precious faculty and one which has won more battles than anything else: but though I have tried to acquire it, my efforts have failed, and I fear it is a sense we are born with or born without and one which no manner of striving can ever produce.

Being, then, very conscious of this failing, I hastily reviewed the position which I meant, if I could, to set up: but, always provided that the failure of the lamp aroused no sort of suspicion, I could find no fault in my plan.

When he had tested the switch, the sentry would grope for a chair, with the object of reaching the lamp. Until he had removed and replaced this and then again tested the switch, I did not believe that he would arouse his sergeant, for no one likes being awakened without just cause, and the ordinary army sergeant is no sucking-dove.

Of moving the lantern from the trestle I had no fear. Its light was feeble, and, since its sides were not glazed, but only its face, and since its face was looking towards the bridge, no one that stood in the loggia could have told if it were burning or no. I could therefore move it wherever I pleased, so long as I kept its face turned from the guard-room porch.

With an earnest prayer that the sentry would stay where he was, I stole back the way I had come...

This simple reconnaissance took much less time to make than it has taken to tell, and I waited five minutes at the corner before I was aware of the Rolls. Of her approach I heard nothing, and when I saw her first she was only six feet away. This looked well for our venture, for the guard-room was no further than the corner from the turbulent fall, and moreover, while the sentry was unready, I had been expecting the car.

At once I told Bell to find me a pair of wire-cutting pliers, and, whilst he was getting them out, I told the Grand Duchess my plan.

"But if the sentry sees you," she said. "What if he turns and sees you when you are cutting the wire?"

"I shall go on and cut it," I said. "Plunged into sudden darkness, what can he do?"

"He can call the guard," says she.

"Let him," said I. "And make the confusion worse. They'll only fall over each other, and I shan't wait. You cannot fire at a man if you can neither see him nor hear where he is."

She put a hand to her head.

"I do not like it," she said. "I am afraid. I know you will do no violence, because you have promised me so. But you are inviting violence, and the trigger of a sentry's rifle is very light. If he makes a mistake he is always forgiven for firing, but never for withholding his fire."

"I give you my word," said I, "that I will wait for my chance. I will wait for my chance if I have to stand there for an hour."

"And that, if your chance does not come, you will not make the attempt."

"Yes."

Here Bell gave me the pliers, which seemed to be fairly sharp.

Then I told him to enter the car and to bring her around the corner, until he could see the trestle from end to end. He did so carefully.

"Now," said I, "I am going to put out that light. The moment it disappears, take the car over the bridge. Wait there and watch the lantern. If it moves, you'll know that all's well: and when you see it down on the edge of the road, *but not before that*, take the car past the guard-room as quick as you can. When you're fifty yards by, switch on your side and tail lamps and let her go. If need be, use your engine. When you've gone about half a mile, put out your lights and wait by the side of the road. Now is all that perfectly clear?"

"Yes, sir," said Bell.

I turned to the Grand Duchess.

"Will you come with me?" I said.

Together we crossed the bridge.

"Now," said I, "I would like us to go together up to the loggia's wall. When the moment comes, I shall leave you and go over that wall. The instant the light goes out, slip past the steps. I shall be on the steps myself, and I shall not move from them until I have heard you go by. The moment you are clear of the guard-room, run like the wind: but keep close against the wall until the car has gone by. Don't look back for the lantern, for its face will be turned from you, and there will be nothing to see."

A moment later we were standing beneath the loggia's wall.

The sentry was as I had left him, with his back towards us and his arms on the top of the wall. The man was short of stature, and I think that the height of the wall must have suited him very well, enabling him to rest his body so far as it could be rested without he sat down. That this was the reason why he maintained his posture I have no doubt, but at the moment I had no room for speculation, but only for thankfulness.

As I was peering, I felt the Grand Duchess' hand slip into mine.

For a moment I held it close.

Then –

"I shall stay on the steps," I breathed, "until you go by."

An instant later I was up and over the wall. It was an anxious moment, for the switch was some twelve feet distant, and had the sentry turned, I do not know what I should have done. But Fortune was with me. The man stood still as death, while, pliers in hand, I covered the fateful distance as smoothly as any shade.

A foot above the switch was a staple pinning the wire to the wall. Above this the wire hung slack. I cut it clean directly above the staple, and almost leaped with surprise at what I had done.

As the sentry swung round with an oath, I slipped to the steps, and, as he made for the switch, the Grand Duchess went by.

I heard the snap of the switch and then a grunt of disgust. Then the fellow fouled the door of the guard-room, and somebody spoke.

And that was as much as I heard, for at that moment I took up the little lantern to set it down in the road.

Its case might have been red-hot.

I have no excuse to offer, for only a fool would have done such a foolish thing, but at least I paid for my folly in anguish of body and mind.

I do not know how I held it, except that the pain was less dreadful than the fear of letting it fall, but I smelled my own flesh roasting, and my fingers were scarred for months.

The trestle was very heavy, but I think that I could have moved it had it been twice its weight.

Then I returned for the lantern and, wrapping it in my handkerchief, removed it to the edge of the road.

As I looked up, the sentry lighted a match.

He was standing upon a chair, and I think he was wishing to find the electric lamp.

The match flared for a moment and then went out. As it did so, the Rolls swept by with the swoop of a bird.

I thought the man must have noticed the movement of air, but he uttered no sound, and, as I turned to follow, he lighted another match.

I was sorry for the fellow, for I knew it would go hard with him when the trestle was found to be moved, and, after all, he had fairly done his duty, and I had only passed him by means of a trick. Indeed, for his sake, I would have put back the trestle, but that would have been to run a wanton risk and, even so, I could not have mended the wire, which must presently speak for itself.

Perhaps twenty yards from the guard-room the village began. As I passed the first house, a slight figure fell in beside me without a word.

"Much ado about nothing," said I, dropping into a walk. "And, by the by, if you had obeyed your orders, you'd be a furlong from here."

"Did you think that I would leave you?" she said.

We passed through the tiny village and into a widening valley with mountains on either side. Far in the distance there was a pinprick of light.

The Grand Duchess raised her arm.

"That's the level-crossing at Vardar. We turn to the right there, and five miles further we'll strike the Vigil road."

At her mention of Vigil my heart sank down like a stone.

That this was out of all reason I know very well, but yet I think it was natural, because I loved her so much. For twenty-four hours I had had sole charge of my darling: for twenty-four hours I had been her familiar friend: I had sat beside her, seen her smile flash for me, breathed the breath of her lips. And now all that was over. Within the hour we should be back in our places, and God alone knew whether we ever should leave them again.

"I took you," I said suddenly. "I should have been ashamed if I could not have brought you back."

"Is that why you risked your life?"

"I never did that," said I.

"We won't argue the point," said she. "Is that why you climbed the wall and cut the wire?"

"I don't know," I said slowly. "I suppose so. We had to get by. But, now that we've done it – well, you try to break out of a prison, but we seem to have broken in." I laughed rather wretchedly – I do not know why. "Of course it's all part of the game, but I – I wish to God I was taking you, instead of bringing you back."

The Grand Duchess stopped in her tracks.

"Oh, my dear, *why didn't you?*" she said.

For a moment we looked at each other. Then my world seemed to stagger, and when it was steady again, I was holding her close to my heart, and her arms were about my neck…

"Oh, Leonie, I love you," I breathed. "I – "

"I know. I'm so glad, my darling. Why didn't you take me away?"

"Because I'm a fool – a madman. Because – "

"Because you're honest," she said. "I tried so hard to make you – twice I tried. Once when we'd left the bridge and again at the top of the pass. A thousand men out of a thousand would have done it, but because you're so honest it never even entered your mind."

What I said I cannot remember, but I know that I tried to show her that she was doing me honour that I did not deserve and that, after a little, we seemed to be in agreement that, cost what it might, my duty was to bring her to Vigil, and that when I burst out in the orchard I was not myself.

When I had kissed her, she took my face in her hands.

"Why do you love me?" she said. "You know that I am out of your reach and you cannot tell why I am fighting to save Paul's throne."

"I love to serve you," said I. "The future can take thought for itself."

"Ah," says she. "The future."

A shiver ran through her body and I held her more close than before.

"But you will remember," she said, "that if you had taken me away, I should never have loved you so well."

"I will remember, Leonie."

"Always – whatever happens – for the rest of your life."

"Always."

Then she gave me her lips, and, after a little, we made our way to the car.

Forty-five minutes later we stood in the hall of the house of the Countess Dresden of Salm.

That lady was speaking.

"Yesterday, just after lunch, the Prince had another stroke. Everyone thought he was dying: but at three o'clock he rallied. He's still himself, but very much shaken and changed. Sully is greatly perturbed. It seems that, when he rushed to the palace, the sentries didn't know him or something, and *he had great difficulty about getting in.*"

There was nothing to be said, and after a moment or two I took my leave.

By the time that I reached the flat it was two o'clock.

All was quiet and in darkness, but I went into Hanbury's bedroom, to tell him that I was back and to give him my serious news.

The room was empty, and the bed was untouched. I went to the other rooms, but neither George nor Rowley was in the flat.

Presently I roused the butler.

He told me that they had gone out some five and a half hours ago: he had an idea, he added, that George had received some summons, for they had left hastily and, just before their going, he had heard the telephone bell.

7

The Four Footmen

I think it was natural that I should be greatly concerned.

The Countess Dresden would have told me if she had spoken with George, and I did not think it like Sully to use the telephone. The message, then, could hardly have come from a friend. Now George was no fool. If he had indeed gone out as the result of a message from someone he did not know, the summons must have been such as he dared not ignore. It seemed to me unpleasantly likely that my name had been taken in vain. If someone had spoken from a distance, saying that I was in trouble and giving George Hanbury a message which purported to come from me, be he never so suspicious, he would have had no option but to obey the call. I reflected dismally that my lady was perfectly right. We were not safe in Vigil: Johann had made up his mind to cut our claws.

I made my way into the loggia and stood looking out into the night.

Once again the sense of helplessness bore down what spirit I had. If George did not reappear, what could I do?

I supposed that I should try to find him – I who was pledged myself to disappear before the next sun had set...

Perhaps because I was weary, the hopelessness of our venture stood out very stark and grim. There was no health in it, but only vanity and peril and vexation of heart. The Grand Duchess' home was gone, George Hanbury was missing, and my darling and I had together been shown a happiness, which had for me killed all other, which could never be ours.

Bell came to say that he had served me some supper, but I had no appetite and bade him go to his bed.

Without a word he left me, to return with a glass of champagne.

To decline an attention so marked would have been churlish, so I thanked him and drank the wine.

" 'Double, double toil and trouble'," said I, and set the glass down on the tray.

"I think you should eat, sir," said Bell. "Her ladyship – "

"What of her ladyship?" said I.

"Her ladyship hoped, sir," said Bell, "that you would make a good meal."

"I will try," I said abruptly. And then, "When was this?"

At the top of the pass, sir, while you were gone on ahead. Her ladyship spoke of your strength, sir, and said that nothing could withstand it, except yourself."

Now Bell was a hotbed of loyalty and brought up this unjust saying as though it were gospel truth; and because, I suppose, there is no cordial so rare as the news that another ranks you more high than you know you deserve, I confess with some shame that my spirits began to rise and I saw the manifest wisdom of taking both food and rest.

I therefore went to table and sat down to my lonely meal, while Bell, who refused to leave me, served me better than any butler, and presently, finding that my hand was injured, insisted on greasing my fingers and binding them up.

"And now," said I, rising at last, "you are to have your supper and go to bed. Tomorrow at eight we must try the nearest garage and see if Mr Hanbury has hired a car."

"Let me save you the trouble," said George, coming into the room.

With his words the door of the flat was shut, and, before I could answer, he turned and called to Rowley to put out a change of clothes.

Now Hanbury's news was of so much interest and value that I cannot do better than set down his tale as he told it, using, so far as I can recall them, his very words.

"Since you've been gone we've had an exciting time. Some people might call it sensational – but you shall judge for yourself.

"At eight o'clock yesterday morning a certain agitation suggested trouble of some sort in or about Grieg's flat. Presently Rowley comes in and tells me the truth. Grieg's flat had been entered the night before by some person or persons unknown. No, it wasn't me – I only wish it had been. I've always said that Grieg had a written warrant for all he did and that, if we could only produce it, Johann would be tied and bound. Johann, no doubt, thought the same, and when he learned that we had the flat beneath Grieg's, *he felt it was time to get that document back*. Hence the housebreaking. Grieg's table-drawers were forced and his papers were all over the place. Grieg is not fit to be told, and nobody else has any idea what's missing, so there we are. What breaks my heart is that *I heard the thief*. At least I assume it was he, and, for what it was worth, I told Rowley to make this known. I'd risen to drink some water – I think that wine held the secret of everlasting thirst – at three o'clock, and I heard a step on the gravel outside the house. With true conceit, I imagined that whoever it was had been set to watch me; but though the windows were open the shutters were shut, so I wished him luck of his duty and went back to bed. If only I'd known…

"Well, that was a bad beginning.

"For thinking of what I had missed, I couldn't sit still. I spent the morning afoot, and after luncheon I ranged the streets of Vigil till Rowley was ready to drop. Finally I entered a café – at least I sat down outside – and gave him some beer. It was in the König Strasse, and, as it was only just five, there was plenty of room. Our seats, being on the pavement, commanded an excellent view of all the traffic and particularly of some workmen who were down on their knees in the roadway by the side of a hole. I tell you those men amazed me. They were fine, lusty fellows and full of cheer, and they took no more notice of the traffic than the sheep takes of the crow that sits on its back. The traffic went round and about them as a stream flows round a boulder that breaks its flow, but, though they had no barriers and none of them kept a look-out, they might have been lounging in the midst of some private park. I've never seen such detachment in all my life. Presently I called a waiter and asked what they meant, for so far as I could see they did nothing but roar with laughter and look down the hole. He said at once that they were sewermen and were waiting for one of their number to reappear.

"Now observe the working of Fate. My mind is directed to sewers – not an aristocratic subject, but a highly practical one. At that very moment Rowley touches my arm. 'Look, sir,' says he. I look – to see a man in a car, blocked for a moment by traffic six paces from where we sit. The car was closed, but the man was sitting forward, and I could see his face. It was the face of a man who was worried out of his life – a man sunk deep in trouble, if not despair. More. *It was the face of Sully*.

"Well, Sully desperate could only mean one thing. Things were moving at the palace and moving devilish ill. Your prophecy came into my mind. I wondered whether Sully had been turned from the palace doors...

"In that instant the car moved on and in my mind the connection of thought was made. Sewers...underground ...*access to the palace like that*.

"Well, we followed the car, which very luckily stopped in a neighbouring street. Sully got out and went into a good-looking house, which I presently found was a very exclusive club, and five minutes later Rowley took him a note. This ran as follows:

Vital that I should see you. Suggest we should talk in your car – preferably after dark. Please ring up 979 any time after six appointing a time and place at which you can pick me up.

"For four hours I sat in this flat, sweating and grunting and generally losing weight. Then at last he rang up... Twenty minutes later I was inside his brougham and Rowley was couched in some bushes against my return.

" 'Is the Prince yet alive?' said I.

" 'Yes,' said Sully. 'But he very nearly died at a quarter past two.'

" 'Have you seen him?' said I.

"Sully nodded.

" 'I saw him at half past three. He is very much changed. He certainly knew me, but he can hardly speak. He has held his last Council. If he lives for a year, he will never do business again.'

" 'He won't live for a year,' said I.

" 'They give him two or three days.'

" 'His seizure,' said I, 'took place at a quarter past two: yet you never saw him till half past three.'

" 'That's right,' said Sully slowly. 'I – I was kept in the vestibule. I have reason to think that, *if His Royal Highness had died, I should not have been suffered to pass.*'

" 'Exactly,' said I, and, with that, I unfolded my dream.

"Nearly all palaces have bolt-holes – secret, underground passages, emerging in a cellar or somewhere without the palace grounds. The idea is that, in case of revolution, the King shall have a way of escape. Now this may well be denied, but it happens to be a hard fact. I know of one such passage running out of a palace you've passed a good many times and I know the very house into whose cellar it runs. Very well. The trouble is this. These tunnels are like fire extinguishers. They're installed as a precaution: fifty years go by without a fire, and when the fire does come, nobody knows how to use them, or even perhaps where they are. For one thing the servants have changed…

"When I told Sully that there was a secret passage, he gave me the lie direct.

" 'Nothing doing,' said I. 'Of course you don't know of it. Very likely it isn't known by the Prince himself. Possibly no one knows. But I'll lay you any money the passage is there.'

" 'But if we can't find it,' said Sully.

" 'We must try,' said I. 'The most likely man to know is an old, trusty servant whose father was a servant before him, or someone like that.'

"Sully fingered his chin.

" 'I can think of no one,' he said, 'but the sergeant-footman – Grimm. The Prince's person is practically in his charge. He has four under-footmen, and those five share the duties of ministering to the Prince. No other servants enter the private apartments of which they have charge. I have known Grimm for thirty-five years, and he certainly succeeded his father, who died about twelve years ago.'

" 'The very man,' said I. 'Can you see him at once?'

" 'Yes,' said Sully. 'I can. But I tell you frankly I think that we shall draw blank. Still, this afternoon has shown me that I am out of my depth, and to anyone who thinks that he can touch bottom I am ready to hand my staff.'

" 'If,' said I, 'there is a passage at all, it runs out of the royal apartments. Consider, then, what such an entrance is worth. Once you are in, your presence – '

"With a look of unutterable distress, Sully threw up his hands.

" 'Kneller has failed me,' he said. 'He knew that I was detained, but he never interfered. I am not sure of the physicians, the Prince is past speaking, and, except for Grimm, there is no one in the palace that I trust. And all without are sitting upon the fence.'

" 'Find me the passage,' said I, and left it there.

"We drove to where we'd left Rowley, and I got out.

"I expected that Sully would be gone for an hour and a half, and, when his car reappeared in forty minutes, I was prepared for the worst. I thought that he had again been refused admission and that the Prince was dead.

"I was quite wrong.

"He'd been to the royal apartments and seen the Prince. What was more to the point, he'd seen Grimm…

"*There's a passage leading out of the wardrobe, adjoining the Prince's room. It runs underneath the gardens, and its exit is in the old fosse which runs down into the river about half a mile from here.*

"Whereabouts in the fosse Grimm didn't know, and that's why Rowley and I got so devilish wet. In the end we found it, under a bridge.

"It's very cleverly done, and if I hadn't been looking, I should have gone clean by it ten times out of ten. For one thing, the fosse is hardly a thoroughfare, and for another, who ever looks under a bridge? If you do, what do you see? A niche in the wall. A niche some six feet high by four feet deep, with ferns growing in and around it and good enough for a statue you want to forget. I damned near gave it a miss…

"Well, the mouth of the passage is in the side of the niche. I'd expected a door of some sort, and, after a dozen paces, I came to an old iron gate. This we managed to force, and *less than an hour ago I was talking to Grimm.*

"He's a stout old fellow is Grimm.

"Directly Sully learned that there *was* a passage, he had the wit to tell Grimm why he wanted to know and to bid him stand by to expect me during the night. Grimm sent the footmen to bed and himself lay down in the wardrobe with his ear to the floor. The rest was easy…

"Two nuns are nursing the Prince, but they've neither eyes nor ears, and they never go further than the bathroom where they take it in turns to rest. There are three physicians in attendance, two of whom sleep in the palace and are hand in glove with Johann. Grimm would not trust his footmen out of his sight. One of them – yes: he's his son. But the other three – no. If Duke Paul appeared in the bedchamber the news would be through the palace in five minutes' time. As for letting them know of the passage…

"It follows that there's only one moment at which the passage can be used – when the Prince is *in extremis*. At that most important moment the Grand Duchess, Sully and Duke Paul must use it to reach their posts. The sight of them may stiffen Kneller and it ought to shake up Johann.

"Well, there you are. We now have access to the palace – private, unsuspected access which a child of four could employ. The fosse is full of bushes, and a path like a sheep-run makes its way down to the niche. There a little step-ladder might help. But that, of course, is a detail. Access we have. Sully will see the Grand Duchess tomorrow as soon as he can. Then she will ring up for the Rolls, and Rowley, when he gets there, will tell her our news. He'll tell her how to get to the passage, and admission to the wardrobe can be fixed between Sully and Grimm. It's a step in the right direction: but it isn't command of the palace by a very long chalk. You can fill the wardrobe with soldiers, but, if they won't do as you tell them, they're better away. By using the passage Sully will draw a good trump: but, unless such a loss makes Johann throw in his hand – and unless he's a very cheap guy, I don't quite see why it should – well, the sweep's got two or three others to carry him home.

"And now let's hear your news." He pointed to my bandaged hand. "That suggests that it's meaty, and I'm sure the wallah that did it is sorry he spoke."

Beside so brilliant an achievement the tale of my adventures seemed very small beer, and the War Office order which we had been shown at Elsa furnished the only light which I was able to shed upon the state of affairs.

By the time my tale was over, George had eaten and drunk, and, since we were both very tired, it seemed best to postpone all discussion and go to our beds, "for, as I have told you," said I, "after tonight we shan't sleep in them any more, and God only knows when and where we shall lay our heads."

Reviewing the position next morning, no one could have pretended that the outlook was good. Thanks to George Hanbury's exploit, our cause was no longer hopeless: but that was all.

The Prince was undoubtedly dying. It was not to be so much as imagined that he could survive till August when Johann's command would be up. At the crucial moment, therefore, Johann would be in the palace and commanding the Body Guard.

The Grand Duchess, Sully and Grimm stood entirely alone. The Countess Dresden could do nothing, and her husband was on a mission to some other court. Even Kneller, the general whom Sully had specially summoned to strengthen his arm, had proved a broken reed.

On the other hand Johann was powerful within and without. He had command of the palace, and the War Office plainly was ready to do as he said. The Household and Privy Council were under his mailed hand. The Lord President might protest, but four hundred men-at-arms were ever a formidable answer to any argument.

Parliament there was none. Riechtenburg was governed by the Prince in Council – and the Councillors were sitting on the fence. That they had been suborned was unlikely: rather they had thought for themselves and, observing the quarter from which the wind was setting, were proposing to take their orders from whoever was in a position to have his orders obeyed. I had no doubt whatever that Church and State would follow the Councillors' lead.

Johann had the whip-hand.

When the moment came he would have to outface the Grand Duchess and Sully, too. I did not envy him his task. But, though his ears might burn, he would stand his ground. And when they had said their say, Johann would turn to Duke Paul – *and show him the whip…*

Now this was surmise, but I had a presentiment of a struggle that would be still-born, because the heir apparent would himself deliver his birthright into his enemy's hand.

The Grand Duchess telephoned herself at a quarter to ten o'clock.

"Good morning," she said. "I am told I am to order the car."

"I will send it at once," said I.

"I should like to see you," she said, "and, since you are going away, I cannot see any harm in the two of you coming to lunch."

"We shall be very happy," said I.

"At one o'clock, then. Goodbye."

The Grand Duchess' words brought us face to face with a problem which we had not yet tried to solve.

That night we must go into hiding. We must give our butler notice and quit our flat: we must go to the station, register most of our baggage and take the Salzburg train. To leave the train surreptitiously should not be hard, but we did not know the country and we had but a rough idea of the cover which it would afford. Unless we were close to Vigil, we might as well be in Wiltshire, for all the help we could give. The servants must be able to find us, yet how could we tell them where to seek us when we knew no more than they did where we should be? Over all, the pressure of time hung like a thundercloud. The Prince was moribund. Unless, as I had promised, a message could always reach us at the outside within the hour, we could be of no more service than the seventy-seven statues about the cathedral doors.

I am ashamed to say that we wasted an hour and a half seeking the answer to this riddle, when all the time it was staring us in the face. Indeed, I can never again despise the bumble-bee that dashes his burly body against one window-pane, while another, directly beside it, is open wide.

We had but to take the train which left after dark, alight from it quietly before it had gathered speed and privily repair to the passage which George had found.

I think it is manifest that, had we sought for a year, we could never have found a retreat one half so convenient from every point of view; and I found great comfort in reflecting that, when Death came to the palace, we should be ready and waiting to usher my lady and Sully into the presence and that, once we had done so, we could remain within call.

Without more ado, we thereupon summoned the butler and told him that we must leave Vigil that very night. We had, we said, business in England to which we must instantly go, only spending a day at Salzburg to take up some gear. The poor man seemed quite overwhelmed by this sudden change in our plans, for he and his wife had spared no pains to make us comfortable and, being both excellent servants, I think preferred our service to sitting with their hands in their laps. At once he protested that he must return us some money, because we had used the apartment for less than a week, yet had paid a month's rent in advance, and then went off to check the wine and provisions which he had bought, that he might give us due credit for all that we had not consumed: indeed, it was most disconcerting to see so troubled by his honesty a man whom once we had suspected of playing his master false.

However, upon reflection, we called him back and told him to put up his pencil and let the arithmetic go, for that, if he had no objection, we proposed to leave Bell and Rowley under his care and the Rolls in the garage which suited her very well; "for," said George, "as you have probably heard, the three are serving the Grand Duchess Leonie, and, apart from the trouble of finding them other lodging, they are very much better here than anywhere else."

Here Bell and Rowley returned and made their report.

They had spoken with the Grand Duchess, who had said that the Prince was no worse, and then had proceeded, as usual, to take up Duke Paul. The Grand Duchess had decided to visit some shops, but the Duke had flatly refused to enter the crowded streets, and when Bell, who was driving, had not obeyed his orders to go about, had lost control of himself and had tried to get out of the car. They had, thereupon, turned round and had driven along by the river and through the Park, but had found these quarters deserted except for nursemaids and children, as was only to be expected at that time of day.

There was nothing to be said, so we told them the plans we had made and set them to packing our clothes; but the stars in their courses seemed to be fighting against us, for the only explanation of the Duke's demeanour was that his nerve was broken and that he feared the people whom he was hoping to rule.

Here I may say that by now we had all four taken to carrying arms: this by no sort of arrangement, but because first one occasion and then another had seemed to demand the precaution, and, once it was taken, I suppose we saw no good reason to lay it aside.

It was now midday, and we were to lunch at one.

Now, happy as I was to be going to see my lady, I had no sooner accepted her invitation than I began to doubt the wisdom of visiting her at all.

On the face of it, such a visit was harmless enough; but the time was out of joint, and the measures which we had taken in the hope of setting it right were highly irregular. Though there was nothing to show it, both George and I were marked men, and the constant use of our car by so great a personage must have occasioned comment. Johann, who knew the truth, was out for blood. If he could turn our acquaintance to her embarrassment – link her name, for instance, to some scandal which he had trumped up, he would do so in a moment of time.

I had an uneasy feeling that by lunching with the Grand Duchess we were playing the enemy's game.

By my desire, therefore, we made our way into the town and sat for a quarter of an hour beneath the awning of a café in one of the principal streets. At the end of that time we rose and stepped into a taxi which was crawling by the side of the kerb, shouting the address of our flat for such as had ears to hear: but, when we had turned two corners, we told the driver to take us to the Bridge of St Anne. This was an aged structure, crooked and roofed, and could not be used except by foot-passengers, of whom I fully expected that we should meet very few. In fact, we met none at all, and, since the Lessing Strasse lay but a stone's throw away from the farther end of the bridge, I had a good hope that we had covered our tracks.

Luncheon was over, and the Grand Duchess and I were walking in the pleasant garden under the tall trees. The Countess and Hanbury were sitting upon the terrace, and George was talking lightly and making her laugh.

"What is your name?" said my lady. "Your Christian name? Mr Hanbury calls you 'Bill,' but I do not like that."

"My names are 'Richard William', Leonie."

"Richard," said she. "You were named for an English King."

"Oh, no," said I. "It's a very common name."

"I do not find it common," she said.

I folded my arms.

"I kiss the lips that said that, Leonie."

She turned a glowing face.

"They are yours, Richard."

"I know," said I. "I cannot believe it. Why do you love me, my dear?"

"No man can see himself, Richard. If you could, you would understand."

"I have a looking-glass."

"Which tells you nothing," she said. "If you met yourself in the street, you would not know who it was."

The thing was too hard for me, and I let it go.

She was, as ever, most smartly yet simply dressed. And, unless I am much mistaken, she was wearing the little slippers that I had cleaned so gladly the day that I fell in love.

"I am mad about you," I said uncertainly. "I have lived last night over again a thousand times."

She cupped her sweet face in her hands.

"So have I, Richard. I asked you to lunch because I – Oh, my darling, I had to see you again."

The blood was coming into my head, and I forced my eyes away from her perilous beauty and strove with all my might to steady my voice.

"I cannot go on," I said thickly. "I cannot speak of these things and not hold you against my heart. I am sorry, but I – I have never loved anyone before, and I cannot go on."

"Nor I, Richard, nor I. I have never loved anyone else, and I never shall. It was always my terrible fear that I should fall in love. I used to pray to be delivered, morning and night. And now – oh, my dear, what shall I do? We may be speaking together for – for almost the very last time. I cannot explain, but my part is written down, and I must play it out."

"So is mine now," I muttered, and did not know my own voice. "I will play it faithfully."

"Say that you love me, Richard. Say you will always love me, whatever I have to do."

With my nails biting into my palms, I addressed the foliage above.

"I love you," I said shakily. "I dare not look at your beauty, because I love you so much. But that does not matter, because I know it so well. Your hair and your white throat and the light in your glorious eyes. From head to heel you are peerless, and I shall have eyes to see no other woman so long as I live."

"Richard, Richard!"

With the tail of my eye, I could see that her hands were trembling against her cheeks and that she was pressing her temples so that the blood had run back from her fingernails.

"Hush, darling," said I. "We must not talk of these things. The good God will give us another time."

For all my preaching, she was the first to have herself in hand.

"The passage," she said presently, "will make you a very hard bed."

"We can take rugs with us," said I. "Besides, I have lain in worse places and done very well."

"At least," she said, "it will not be for long. A day or two at the most. And you will be safe there, and – and I rather dread the business and I shall be very glad to know that you are so near."

"I shall be in the wardrobe," said I. "If – "

"No, no," she cried. "No, no." She caught my arm. "Whatever happens, you must not leave the passage. A stranger in the royal apartments would be shot down like a dog. You – "

Here came a step on the gravel, and we turned to see Madame Dresden hastening over the grass.

"What is it, Marya?"

"Sully is here," said the Countess.

"So soon?" breathed the Grand Duchess. A hand went up to her throat. Then, "Come," she said, and led the way to the house.

I was as certain as she that Sully was come to say that the end was at hand, and to tell the truth, I was confounded, for I am not a man that can move quickly, but like to be able to follow some preconceived plan. Such a plan I had made already, and I think it is here convenient to set it out.

Any change in the Prince's condition was telephoned to Sully by Grimm. When the latter had reason to think, that the Prince was sinking, *before apprising Sully* he was in future to telephone to Rowley and Bell, who would be waiting his message by day and night. Upon receipt of this call, Rowley and Bell would instantly turn out the Rolls, take up the Grand Duchess and the Countess and then Duke Paul and bring the three to the passage as swiftly as ever they could. There Sully would meet them, for his house, it appeared, was but eight minutes' walk from the fosse; and there George and I would be ready to take them in.

The fault in this plan is as evident as it was gross. Like a fool, I had taken it for granted that the Prince would live until midnight, or at least until we had taken the Salzburg train…

"I have come from the palace," said Sully. "The Prince is not sinking, but he is very weak. He tried to give me some directions, but the strain was too great. I went there by arrangement, your Highness. As you know, I now go by arrangement three times in the day." He paused there, in evident distress. "Had I waited to be summoned, madam, I should have waited in vain. *Grimm's telephone is not working. He has been unable to use it since ten o'clock.*"

For a moment there was dead silence.

Then Hanbury spoke.

"Grimm can use another line."

"If he leaves the apartments," said Sully, "he fears that he may not get back. There are sentries everywhere."

"But he has to leave for his food."

Sully shook his head.

"No. The royal apartments are like an ordinary flat. Grimm and the four footmen sleep and eat next to the Prince. They always have. A lift goes down to the kitchens. For the last three days neither Grimm nor his son have been out of the royal apartments."

"What of the others?" said I. "The other footmen, I mean?"

Sully shrugged his shoulders.

"They are untrustworthy. Grimm has reason to think that one at least was aware that the telephone was to be cut. He would dismiss them in an instant, but they are kept so busy that they cannot be spared."

149

The Countess put in her oar, but I was trying to think and I do not know what she said.

The loss of the telephone was serious: but, once we were in the passage, one of us could act as a runner to carry the news. What was, to my mind, far more grave was that *three out of five of the men who were in the holy of holies were taking their cue from Johann*.

Sully was speaking.

"If we are not to be advised, madam, we stand no chance. I cannot dwell at the palace, and even if I could – "

"Are the footmen powdered?" said I.

They all stared at me.

"Yes," said Sully. "The Prince always keeps his state."

"Tell me," said I. "At what hour do you go there again?"

"At six o'clock," said Sully.

I glanced at the watch on my wrist.

"In three and a half hours' time. Can you go there before?"

"I would rather not," said Sully. "I have no doubt that my visits are reported to the Duke Johann. I do not wish him to find them irregular."

"Then must we hope," said I, "that the Prince's condition will not change before six o'clock. At that hour give Grimm these orders. First, he is to sack the three footmen he does not trust – return them to ordinary duty, or, if they have no other, send them away. This he is to do then and there. Let them change their clothes and be gone by seven o'clock. And when they are gone, he will go at once to the wardrobe, open the door to the passage and speak to George."

Sully put a hand to his head.

"But I have told you, Chandos, that Grimm says they cannot be spared. The apartments are spacious, and the men are on their feet from – "

"I will replace them," said I. "All three – at seven o'clock."

There was an electric silence.

Then I heard a sound which sent my heart into my mouth.

It was the clear, peremptory call which Duke Paul had sounded at Anger against my will – a call not meant for cities, but used to clear the way on the open road.

It was the horn of the Rolls.

I turned to the Grand Duchess.

"I hear the servants," I said. "They were not told to come here, and they would never have done so without good cause. I beg that you will excuse us, and please induce Baron Sully to do as I say."

She was very calm, but I saw the alarm in her eyes.

"You should have left Vigil this morning."

"Oh, no," said I, smiling. "You won't forget Grimm's orders? At seven o'clock."

My darling looked me full in the eyes.

"I shall forget nothing," she said.

The next instant I was gone.

I followed George out of the hall and closed the front door.

As I did so, the Rolls came to rest by the pavement beyond the gate.

Two men, standing on the pavement, were watching it curiously: then they glanced at each other and turned to the steps.

"Not a moment to lose, sir," said Rowley, as though he were speaking to Bell.

As we passed through the gate –

"Excuse me, sirs," said one of the plain-clothes police, "but, if I may ask your indulgence – "

"Another time," said George.

He brushed the fellow aside and vaulted into the car.

Another car was turned violently into the quiet street.

"That's them, sir," said Rowley. "Quick!"

As I flung myself forward, the two men fell upon me, as dogs on a rat.

There was no time to repulse them: there was no time for Rowley to come to my aid. The police car was thirty yards off: already its brakes were in action, and I saw its near door open and policemen ready to drop.

By a tremendous effort I reached the side of the Rolls.

Rowley's arms went about me, and George caught hold of my wrists.

"Let her go, Bell," he said.

There never was seen such an exit.

Gathering speed, we swept up the Lessing Strasse, three men within the car and three without. I had one foot on the step, and so had one of the police: his fellow had none. Their full weight was upon me, and between them and George and Rowley I was like to be torn in two. Behind us came yells and whistles and the storming of gears.

As we swung round the first corner, the two police tightened their grip. They were holding to me for safety, and I do not know that I blame them, for we were travelling fast.

George Hanbury was speaking.

"Where are you going, Bell?"

"Into the country, sir. The town isn't safe."

"By the Austrian Road?"

"Yes, sir. It's the only one I know."

"Well, turn to the left as soon as ever you can. Swing her round as sharp as you dare."

"Very good, sir."

An instant later the great car heeled to the left, and the three of us swung inboard, because of the pace. As we did so, Rowley lifted and George caught hold of the man whose arms were about my neck.

Why I was not broken in pieces I do not know, for the two police clung to my body as though they were drowning men. With them like leeches upon me, I was dragged, like a sack of provender, over the side of the car; and even then they would

152

not let go, but George and Rowley had fairly to tear them off me before I could move.

"Are you all right, Bill?" said George.

I was sound enough and only short of some skin, but my clothes were in a bad way, for my coat was split to glory and my shirt was hanging in tatters about my breast.

I then crawled on to the seat, but, when the police would have risen, George bade them stay on the floor.

Five minutes later we were clear of the town.

For the next six miles Bell drove as hard as he could, while Rowley watched our prisoners, and George and I studied the map. Then, where the road was lonely, we turned to the left and set ourselves to the business of baffling pursuit. This was easy, for the country was not at all open and there were plenty of roads.

After perhaps forty minutes, high up among the mountains, we found an excellent lair, where a thicket harboured a quarry which had been long disused. From the head of the quarry a man who was looking out could see the road for some distance on either side, and, though such precaution seemed needless, we set Bell there as a sentry, for one so narrow escape was enough for that afternoon and I had no wish again to see my plans crumble before my eyes.

I will not dwell upon the matter, but so long as I live I shall hear that police car coming and the scream of its brakes. It was only its driver's error that saved us both. Had he turned in in front of the Rolls, we should have been trapped. Had he but run alongside, the police could have boarded the Rolls and won their match. But, as I have shown, he did neither – and, as the saying is, a miss is as good as a mile.

Hanbury took out tobacco and started to fill a pipe. Then he looked at our prisoners, who were leaning disgustedly against a boulder watching Rowley lash together their ankles as though they were to be entered for a three-legged race.

"You were asking my indulgence," said George, "and I cut you short. What was it you wanted to say?"

The two looked at one another helplessly.

"Go on," said George pleasantly. "You were only doing your duty, and we've no quarrel with you."

To point this assurance, I offered the two cigarettes, but, though they seemed greatly relieved and bowed their appreciation as well as they could, they were plainly reluctant to give us the information we sought.

"I think," said George, "you owe us an explanation. You did your best to arrest us, and, before we leave the country, we should like to know what we've done."

The two regarded one another.

Then –

"You are leaving the country, sir?" said the one who had spoken to George.

"Well, you don't think we're going back? Tonight we shall cross the frontier and be in Salzburg by dawn."

Upon this false declaration, the fellows opened their mouths.

We were to have been arrested for breaking and entering Grieg's flat.

When we asked why we were suspected, they swore that they did not know; but, after a little, admitted that I was charged with the felony and George with being accessory after the fact.

"I was out of Vigil," said I, "as your masters very well know."

Professional pride will out.

"You were there until midnight, sir: and you left the opera-house at half past nine."

I stared at the speaker.

"That's perfectly true," said I. "Who told you that?"

"Do not ask any more, sir," said the other. "I am sure that you had good reason for all you did, but the warrant was all in order – and, if I may say so, I think you are wise to be gone. You have given offence in high quarters, and – "

"Let me see the warrant," said George.

At once both protested that the warrant had been held by their chief who had gone to our flat to take us, because he had reason to think that we should be there.

George Hanbury fingered his chin.

"I think," said he, "that you have a duplicate. You see, your chief wasn't with you, and, without a warrant…"

He nodded to Rowley, who started to search their pockets in a highly professional way.

"It is hopeless," said one. "Give it him."

A blue envelope passed, and George and I sat down to see what its papers would show.

The warrant was seemingly in order, and we turned to another and longer document.

"By thunder!" cried George. "By thunder, this is the goods. This is the 'information' – the secret depositions upon which the warrant was applied for. No wonder they were so sticky about parting."

There were in all five deponents.

The first was Grieg.

His testimony may be imagined. He swore to the bad blood between us and our attempt upon his life, to our sudden occupation of the flat directly below him and our undoubted desire to do him grave injury.

The second was Grieg's servant.

He swore that our ways were suspicious and that we kept strange hours: that on the night in question he had been out by permission from nine o'clock until twelve: that, though it was not discovered until the morning, he had no doubt that the crime had in fact been committed between those hours, for that he was a light sleeper, yet had heard no sound in the night: that George Hanbury had volunteered that he heard some movement at three, in the hope, no doubt, of diverting suspicion from us.

The third and fourth were detectives, who swore little more than that they knew us by sight and that our ways were peculiar and not at all those of tourists seeking amusement abroad.

The fifth deponent put the rope round our necks.

He swore that we were desperate men and that we carried arms. He had seen us do violence and had heard us threaten Grieg. He had seen us in the stalls of the theatre on Wednesday night and had particularly noticed *that after the first act of Tosca I had gone out of the house and had not reappeared.*

Such was the deposition of his Highness Duke Paul of Riechtenburg.

It is said of Henry II, King of England, that when he saw signed against him his own son's name, John, Count of Mortain, he turned his face to the wall.

We were not thus moved, and, though we were at once dumbfounded and most deeply provoked, I am glad to think that the more we considered the outrage, the less consideration it seemed to deserve.

At first, in our haste, we were ready to return to Vigil and lay the papers before the Grand Duchess herself. But presently reason prevailed, and we remembered that, after all, Duke Paul was no more to us than a chessboard king that we were seeking to move to his proper place.

"Speaking for myself," said George, "this entirely beastly young man can go to hell. I'm helping a pretty lady to – God save her – her heart's desire. I suppose she's in her right mind, but let that go. And if her heart's desire is to cherish a third-class viper – well, we must expect to be bitten whenever we give it the chance."

It was, of course, for my sake that George took the matter so well, for, whatever may be your reason for taking up the cudgels in another's behalf, if he himself turns upon you, it is only human to wash your hands of the business and let him fare as he deserves: but George was the soul of loyalty and, since it was my furrow he was ploughing, nothing but my hesitation would have made him look back.

His parable of the viper was, I fear, much to the point, but it must be remembered that Duke Paul had little or no idea that we were doing our utmost to place him upon the throne: that does not excuse his misconduct, but, as some two hours later, we picked our way through the mountains towards the town we had left, I could not help feeling that to judge such a youth too harshly was easy enough.

The duke was evil, and the blood in his veins was bad. Little wonder that in such soil honesty languished and ill weeds grew apace. I think he liked no one but himself, and I do not think he would ever have been familiar with any honest man. The Grand Duchess he valued, as one treasures a beautiful horse. Us he disliked of instinct. He envied our car and our servants and our freedom from worldly care. We had not courted his pleasure, and more than once we had shown him very plainly that we were not under his orders and would stand no nonsense from him. Before these whips he had been helpless as the shorn lamb before the wind. Finally, he had grown jealous. The Grand Duchess plainly liked us, and when at Barabbas she had been missing and I had gone off to seek her, I remember that his eyes were upon us as we came forth together to enter the car.

That in this matter of the warrant he had been Johann's cats-paw I had no doubt; and though I have never learned the truth, I fancy Duke Paul spoke freely before his servants, and if these were not faithful or did not hold their tongues, I suppose the rest was simple to a man that was ready and active behind the scenes.

It was now near six o'clock, and we were approaching Vigil from a quarter we did not know.

George and Bell and I were wearing overalls which we had bought in a village and fouled in a ditch. Our faces and hands were filthy with oil and grease, and no one, I think, would have known us but for the Rolls. In sacks we had food enough to last us for two or three days.

We three were bound for the passage – to keep our appointment with Grimm at seven o'clock. Rowley was to set us down on the skirts of the town and then withdraw to the country and lay up the Rolls: when this was done, he would return on foot and make his way to the passage as soon as he could.

A farmer we had found was willing to care for the car, and though we were all reluctant to abandon our magic carpet – for that is what she had proved – our brush with the police had, so to speak, put her in balk. She had only to be seen in Vigil to be immediately chased, and, since secrecy was of the essence of the course we were trying to steer, to use her would have been madness, no matter how sore our need.

Now I was far from easy about the walk we must take to reach the fosse. For one thing, we had no map or plan of the streets, and, while it is simple enough to find some prominent feature of any town, the skirts of Vigil were ample and we had no time to spare, yet dared to ask the way of no man, lest such a question should bear us evil fruit: for another, it was broad daylight. Still, the engagement had been made, and I feared that if we did not keep it, Grimm would think we had failed him and shut the door.

My forebodings were justified.

For a full hour we wandered, afraid to loiter, afraid to show undue haste, afraid to consult together, afraid to go different ways, and when at last I glanced through an open house door to look clean through the building and see beyond it the trees of the palace gardens, I could hardly believe my eyes.

At once I told George, who was slouching along, fuming, some two or three paces ahead, and five minutes later we were all looking into the fosse.

The fosse was a natural gorge which many years before had been partly revetted by man. To judge by the ear, water was steadily coursing down all its length, and waterside bushes and plants had come to such luxuriance that at some points the walls were hidden and the fosse was so full of green that none could have told its depth without a sounding-rod. As a matter of fact it was some thirty feet deep, and I think it was something wider, but I cannot be sure. Upon one side ran a pleasant, quiet road with, beyond it, the wall which fenced the palace gardens from curious gaze: on the other, the backs of old houses stood up in some disarray, and I think an artist would have found half a dozen pictures in the little I was able to remark.

Three bridges were spanning the fosse that I could see, all of them weatherbeaten and very elegant, with their piers thick-covered with moss, and lichen on all their stones. The last of the three was marked by a pretty pulpit which rose from its parapet and was meant, I suppose, for a bridge-ward in days gone by: and since George had mentioned this feature, I knew that this was the bridge beneath which the passage emerged.

It had been arranged that we should each enter the fosse at a different place and make our way to the passage by the bed of the stream; and perhaps because I was the most fearful I was the first to disappear.

As luck would have it, there were not many people in sight, but those that were there were of a dangerous kind, for they were about no business but that of strolling and staring and generally taking their ease.

I walked down the road slowly...

Now and again there were little breaks in the wall which was guarding the fosse, and from each of these a path or a rude flight of steps went down very sharp. I afterwards found that these ways led down to old troughs in which the poor women of Vigil had used to wash clothes.

There was no time to be lost: indeed, every moment I was expecting to hear some impatient clock declare the hour: so I laid the sack I was bearing upon the wall and, in taking my seat beside it, struck it as though by accident into the fosse below.

The ruse was slight enough and, for all I know, may have been needless, but it gave me a certain courage, and I started without more ado, to recover my bread and cheese.

A moment later I was hastening along the bed of the busy water, while the bushes which flourished about it hid me from view.

As the clocks of Vigil were striking seven o'clock, I swung myself into the niche; and we were all three in the passage before two minutes were past.

Twenty-five minutes later Hanbury was fighting his way into a scarlet coat, while Grimm's son was teaching Bell to powder my hair.

8

In Sheep's Clothing

I do not know whether it is generally known that if you can change the colour of a man's hair, his own mother may be forgiven for passing him by. I certainly never knew it, and when I came suddenly face to face with George Hanbury powdered, for an instant I thought him a stranger, and that is the plain truth. What is more to the point, he made a splendid footman: and, indeed, I think that no one would ever have suspected that he and Bell and I were not in fact royal servants in all their state.

We were fortunate in our livery, for the sergeant-footman had by him nearly a dozen suits which had been made at one time or another for different men and, being in perfect condition, had been kept against the enlistment of footmen whom they might fit. From these we three were equipped, and though the set of my breeches would perhaps have been questioned in Savile Row, the coats we chose might have been stitched upon us, and no one but we could have told that they were uncomfortably tight.

It will be remembered that we had our food with us: we had, therefore, no need to call upon the kitchens for rations, and since there was nothing to take us beyond the private suite, none of the staff would suspect that the footmen whom Grimm had dismissed had been replaced. The physicians would see us

DORNFORD YATES

and so would the lords-in-waiting, and these would know that
there were still four footmen, while the staff were equally sure
that there was but one: but I judged that with any luck some
time would elapse before these two beliefs came into conflict
and that ere the resultant rumour had won to Johann's ears, the
Prince would be dead.

I, therefore, made up my mind that, provided we bore
ourselves as lackeys, kept our mouths shut and took our cue
from Grimm, we had little to fear: but we spent a broken half-
hour rehearsing the manner we should use on entering and
leaving a chamber, on opening and shutting a door and other
such petty occasions, for, though Grimm and his son were to
shoulder as much of our duty as they could, there was watching
and waiting to be done by night as by day, and, as I shall show,
the service now demanded could not possibly be rendered by
only two men.

The Prince's apartments lay upon the first floor, and, as Sully
had said, they took the form of a flat. This flat was cut from the
rest of the palace by a broad corridor or hall which ran the
width of the building and was laid with a heavy carpet so that
no footfalls might be heard. Immediately beyond this hall lay
the Grand Staircase with a spacious antechamber on either side.
The hall could be reached from either of the antechambers or
from the staircase itself, and I learned that double sentries were
guarding each of these doors. (Myself I heard the guard changed
at nine o'clock.) When I asked if such precaution was usual,
Grimm said that in all his service it had never been taken
before. The back stairs were similarly guarded, and since access
to the private apartments – always an important question – had
now become a matter of the gravest concern, I will deal with it
here and now.

In the ordinary way two footmen were always on duty in the
broad corridor, one at the door from the staircase and the other
at the door of the room in which the Prince happened to be. The

others would be in their quarters or about some other business, while the sergeant-footman himself was always at hand.

There was an unwritten law that no one should ever be admitted to the corridor without reference to the Prince. To this rule there were four exceptions – the two lords-in-waiting on duty, the heir apparent and the Lord President of the Council. Everyone else, however exalted his position or urgent his case, must wait in an antechamber until the Prince's pleasure was known.

In view of the Prince's sickness, this rule had been relaxed so far as the physicians were concerned, and these had immediate access by night or day.

Five days ago, with the connivance of Brooch, the second lord-in-waiting, Johann had been permitted to break this rule, and Grimm had come upon them pacing the corridor. At once he had apprised the Prince, who was much annoyed. Johann had been conducted to an antechamber, and Brooch had been summoned and rated as he deserved.

I think this will show what manner of man Grimm was – strong, fearless and resolute to stand upon his rights. He was answerable to no man, except the Prince. The lords-in-waiting could give him no orders, and the question of access lay with the Prince and with him. If the Prince's pleasure could not be ascertained, the matter rested with Grimm. His personality was compelling. Men were afraid of him, as of the Prince. There was no doubt about it – the old sergeant-footman was a true tower of strength.

For all that, Grimm was a servant, and if Johann chose to crush him, it was within his power. Both of them knew this. But to touch so stout-hearted a man required a purpose which Johann could not summon, and I fancy he waived the matter as one which would lose its importance the moment the Prince was dead. If I am right in this, I think his decision was sound, for with the Prince's death Grimm's authority must plainly fall into abeyance, if not come to an end.

When I asked him whose orders he would take when the Prince had breathed his last, he hesitated a moment and then replied "Those of Duke Paul," but I think he saw that, on the death of a monarch, there must be goings and comings which no one man could control and that, the circumstances being extraordinary, rules and regulations would have to be honoured in the breach.

Grimm's invaluable loyalty had been bred in the bone. He was deeply attached to his master, but he worshipped the latter's office as his father's father had worshipped it seventy years before. In his eyes the succession was sacred. To tamper with the royal tradition was the unpardonable sin. For better or for worse, Duke Paul had been born to the purple – and there was an end of that.

The sergeant-footman was, of course, perfectly right. Maybe his simple outlook was out of date; but so are many honest ways of thinking, and the world would be the richer if there were more spirits of his sort. The man was faithful, cared not at all for himself and, keeping his eyes upon his duty, looked neither to right nor left.

The doctors were lodged in a room which lay directly beneath the royal suite, and, in the event of a crisis, one of the nuns had only to touch a bell to summon them up.

Now, as is the way of an old, commanding nature that has never known a day's sickness for fifty years, the Prince detested the doctors and looked askance at the nuns. He suffered them, because he was helpless, but Grimm was his rod and his staff, and the presence of his old servant comforted him more than all the ministrations of the strangers about his bed. By skilfully exploiting this preference, Grimm had taught the nuns to look upon him as their chief, and I think they told him more than they told the doctors, who were less content to listen than to judge for themselves: since one of the nuns had had much experience of sickness, it follows that Grimm was constantly well informed and knew better than anyone else the actual condition of the patient and the course which his illness was shaping from hour to hour.

Such knowledge was, of course, above price, for unless the Prince were to be taken off by another seizure, the nuns were sure to be able to discern the approach of the end and so to give us that notice of which we had so much need.

At a quarter to nine that evening I took my stand in the hall. My post was at the door of the bedchamber. On the opposite side of the hall young Grimm, half-dead with fatigue, stood to the door from the staircase, with his eyes on the red-glass telltale, which served as a bell. In an easy chair, some twenty paces away, one of the lords-in-waiting was slumbering peacefully.

I have said that I had made up my mind that we had little to fear. So, I think, had we all. But, looking back, I know that this was a fiction by which we sought to cheat our understanding and steady our nerves.

To be perfectly honest, if I had known the nature of the duties which we should have to perform, I should no more have engaged us to undertake them than I would have engaged us to scale the cathedral towers. In my ignorance of the state which royalty keeps, I had imagined that George and Bell and I could watch by night, clean the rooms at cockcrow and hover in the background throughout the day. I had actually wondered what four footmen could find to do. And now, within two hours of my arrival, I was upon parade, at the beck and call of the sleepy lord-in-waiting, who might any moment awake, waiting to usher three doctors into the Prince's room. More. But for the fact that I did not know them by sight, George would have been where I was and I should have been standing at the door which led to the stairs, for, as I have said, young Grimm was at the end of his tether and moved like a man in a dream.

It was, indeed, only the physical exhaustion of himself and his son that had induced the sergeant-footman to consent to adopt my plan. He had done so in desperation and verily believing that, unless he did so, the two would fall asleep standing before six hours were out. "And there," said he, "would have been a nice state of affairs. Not a door in the place I can lock or so much as bolt. The holy women lied to – told I was out of the suite: no one to tell you to send for the Lord Sully: and the corridor full of soldiers before we knew where we were. It's a dreadful thing, sir, to lean on a treacherous crutch."

I had agreed thoughtfully, for I was inwardly wondering what was the difference between a treacherous crutch and a broken reed...

The telltale glowed suddenly, turning its wine-red glass to the colour of fire.

Instantly young Grimm stiffened, and I realized with a shock that the palms of my hands were wet.

I pulled myself together and took a deep breath.

The door was ajar, and young Grimm was looking to see who it was that had 'rung'. Then he stepped back and swung the mahogany wide.

As the physicians entered, I knocked upon the bedchamber's door.

A moment, and this was opened by one of the nuns.

"The doctors?" she whispered.

I nodded, and she let the door go. I set it open at once and stood to one side. As the three physicians passed in, I regarded them carefully. The impulse to look elsewhere or at least to lower my head was most insistent: but it was all important that I should know them again. Two passed me by as though I did not exist, but the third looked me up and down, frowning, till the hair rose upon my head. The truth is, I think, that he mistrusted himself and so sought to allay my suspicion that he found the ways of the mighty in any way strange: but I could have spared his endeavour which seemed to me but the prelude to my denouncement.

Then at last he was gone, and I shut the door.

The visit lasted five minutes, but before they left the sick-room, the lord-in-waiting awoke and strolled up to young Grimm.

"Did I hear the doctors?" he said.

"Yes, my lord."

He was not wearing uniform, and I made up my mind that it was Brooch. It was, of course, mere chance that he had not accosted me.

With the tail of my eye I watched him take out his watch and start to pace up and down...

My door was suddenly opened, and the doctors emerged.

Brooch came to meet them at once.

For a moment or two they stood talking. Then they passed to the door to the staircase, and the janitor opened it wide.

To my inexpressible relief, Brooch followed the doctors out.

"As usual," he said to young Grimm. "If the doctors should have to be summoned, ring also for me."

"Very good, my lord."

The next moment the door was shut.

By one consent, young Grimm and I met together in the midst of the hall.

"Well done, sir," said he. "You see, it is easy enough. Will you know the physicians again?"

"Yes," said I. "Will anyone else come tonight?"

"I do not think so. Possibly General Kneller. Him you can never mistake. His moustache is white and flowing, and he is very bald."

"In uniform?" said I.

"Yes. Azure, by day: by night, the Army blue. But as a General, he always wears a red sash about his waist."

"Will the doctors return?" said I.

"Not till tomorrow morning at nine o'clock."

If only to keep him beside me, I could have questioned the lad for another hour, but to prime me as I should have liked

167

would have taken a week, so he left to fetch George Hanbury, and I took his place by the door that led to the stairs.

When George came, Grimm came with him.

"The Grimms," said George, "are going to take their rest. They won't undress, of course. Bell will be round the corner." He nodded in the direction from which he had come. "From where he stands he can watch the back door as well as the second door of the Prince's room. When the nuns want the sergeant-footman, they always go to that door – not this. If we're in trouble, one of us will have to fetch Grimm."

He spoke in English, but that Grimm understood his last sentence was plain enough.

"No trouble will arise, sir," he said. "I am there, of course, if you need me; but no one will seek admission for another ten hours."

The next moment he was gone.

With my eyes fixed upon the telltale, I took my seat upon a bench, while George fell to pacing the hall.

And here once again George Hanbury's rare intelligence pulled the fat out of the fire.

I fear I should make a bad servant, for I might have viewed disorder a hundred times and never conceived the notion of setting it straight: but George knew better. The chair which Brooch had been using caught his critical eye…

At once he ordered its cushions and folded up the papers which sprawled by its side. As he did so, a pair of spectacles fell to the floor.

I saw George look at them and finger his chin.

Then he came to my side and set them upon a salver which lay on a little table beside my bench.

"Did you see who was there?" he said.

"Brooch," said I.

"Forewarned is forearmed," said he. "He'll be glad of those back."

Half an hour perhaps had gone by, when, to my indescribable horror, the telltale glowed.

I think the sight of that signal – silent, angry, inexorable, took a month from my life.

As George whipped back to his post, I moistened my lips. Then I took a deep breath and opened the door.

Brooch came in, peering.

In a flash I had the salver and was proffering what he had lost.

For a moment he stared at the glasses: then, with a grunt of satisfaction, he picked them up.

"That's right," he said agreeably, blinking up into my face. "It was you that found them last time, wasn't it?"

I dared not reply, but bowed: but he seemed to expect no answer and left at once.

I shut the door behind him and wiped the sweat from my face…

When another half-hour had gone by, but no one had 'rung', I began to dare to hope that until the morning came we should not be disturbed. I, therefore, caught George's eye, and he came to my side.

Hastily we whispered together.

It was no good our looking for Rowley for several hours, for he had some twenty miles to cover on foot, and since one could watch the hall and another was only needed in case Grimm had to be fetched, we arranged that George should lie down and take what rest he could. This, of course, on the carpet and by my side, so that at a touch of my slipper he could be instantly afoot. When he had rested I could lie down in my turn, and when my spell was over one of us could relieve Bell. In this way all three of us would enjoy some relaxation – if you can call it such.

The immediate strain had lessened, but the thought of the morrow made my blood run cold. Grimm and his son would be rested and so better able to keep us in countenance, but the sergeant-footman would be frequently with the Prince, and his son could not be expected never to leave the hall. Even if he stood at the door for twelve hours on end, any moment some crisis might arise which he could not control. The lad was pleasant and was by no means a fool: but he had not the ready wit of Rowley or Bell: what was worse, he would see no danger and smiled at our apprehension that anything might go wrong – *anything…*

For one thing only, one or other of the lords-in-waiting was on duty from nine in the morning till nine at night. And that in the corridor. If he happened to ask us a question, in case our speech should betray us, neither George nor I could reply, while Bell, who knew no German, could not so much as obey the simplest command.

For another, from ten o'clock to midday, distinguished subjects and personal friends of the Prince would be brought to an antechamber, there to learn from the lips of the lord-in-waiting the latest news. For those two hours, therefore, *another door would have to be manned.*

Three doors, not counting the back door – where orderlies would render 'parade states' and copies of the 'orders of the day', and messengers and postmen would deliver dispatches and mails… *Four doors between four footmen, three of whom were play-acting and had never rehearsed their parts.*

These things considered, I think I may be forgiven for, as the saying is, seeing a robber behind every bush.

Over all lowered, as ever, the cloud of Time. How many hours would go by before Johann discovered that the footmen that he had been using had been replaced?

I wrenched my thoughts from the future and turned to the past, and while I remembered the mountains and the cow-bells and the brush of the Grand Duchess' lips, I tried to pretend that the telltale was a tail-lamp which had gone out.

The next day stands out of my memory as high hills stand out at sundown after the rain.

I think any one of us three could set down the whole of its burden, quarter by quarter of an hour, and never make one mistake.

To say that time seemed to drag conveys nothing at all. There were moments when I could have sworn that the clock in the sober hall was standing still. Ten minutes seemed an hour; an hour, eternity: and this unkind illusion far more than doubled the strain which was fretting our nerves.

This was continuously heavy.

We could not take counsel together – each had to act for himself when the moment came: while he sought to foresee some crisis and settle the line he must take, another would spring upon him, demanding immediate action so that the brain boggled at the issues with which it was faced: yet the demeanour of a statue must be deliberately preserved.

For myself, I lived and moved as a man in some frightful dream in which nothing seemed to happen which did not set the nerves tingling or fill the heart with dismay; and, while I am properly ashamed of this disorder, I sinned in good company, for George Hanbury always declares that twice in that day he made up his mind to tell me that he could not go on and that Rowley must be brought from the passage to take his place. This, I think, shows that our plight – which was really more delicate than dangerous – was made to appear more horrid by some malignant means, and I am inclined to lay the blame upon the telltales, for their sudden, noiseless illumination smacked of the supernatural and their sinister likeness to signals of danger was most importunate.

Since, however, the tale of our troubles would fill up a book, I will pass over most of the duty we tried to do and only relate such events as bear upon our endeavour to bring Duke Paul to the throne.

The apartments were swept and garnished by seven o'clock. At that hour, by my request, Grimm opened the door to the passage, and there was Rowley asleep.

He reported that all was well, so I told him to stay where he was and take his ease, holding himself ever ready to seek the Grand Duchess and Sully according to the plan we had laid.

This plan was not at all to my liking, but the devil was driving, and we could think of no better, try as we would.

When the Prince was seen to be sinking, Rowley would run to the Lessing Strasse and give the alarm. At once the Grand Duchess would telephone to Duke Paul. Rowley would run on to Sully's and give him his news and would then repair to Duke Paul's. There he would await the Grand Duchess and Madame Dresden, who, sure to be the first ready, would call for the Duke. Rowley would escort the three to the passage and up to the suite, where Sully would be already, for he had less distance to go.

Such was our miserable scheme. And there I will leave it, for its faults need no pointing out and cannot be diminished by any argument.

At a quarter to nine came Kneller, and at nine the three physicians visited the Prince. They had been gone some ten minutes when Sully arrived.

The Lord President entered quickly, and I saw that his nerves were on edge. Young Grimm admitted him, and I was standing beside the bedchamber's door.

At once Kneller came to meet him and seemed very anxious to please, but Sully, though courteous as ever, was very grave and, while he listened to Kneller, made little or no reply.

So soon as he decently could, he turned to the door upon which I was waiting to knock, but the lord-in-waiting turned with him and the two approached me together, side by side.

This was the last thing I wanted. In Sully's philosophy sensation had no part, and I feared very much that my appearance would discompose my old tutor and that Kneller would remark not only his discomposure, but the source from which it sprang.

I had knocked and was standing, waiting, when I noticed the beads of sweat upon Sully's brow.

My summons was not answered at once, because, I suppose, the nurses were somehow engaged, and the three of us stood together for the longest minute that I have ever known.

Sully stared upon the carpet, I strained my ears for the sound of the nurse's approach, and Kneller put up an eye-glass and surveyed me from head to foot.

I suppose this was natural. The man had held many inspections and had an eye for precision in matters of dress. But his scrutiny was very trying, and I was mortally afraid that he would find something about me which belied the lackey.

At last the door was opened, and Sully passed in.

Kneller turned on his heel and strolled down the hall.

Now it was most important that Sully should be put in possession of the plan I have already set out. It had been arranged, therefore, that when he had seen the Prince, Grimm should conduct him from the sick-room by way of the service door, that so he might speak with George, before returning to the hall by the way he had come. It follows that Sully's reappearance was something delayed, and Kneller, who was waiting to waylay him, more than once glanced at the clock.

At last the door was opened, and Sully emerged.

"Is he speaking?" said Kneller. "I mean – "

"With difficulty," said Sully slowly. "He – he wishes you sworn of the Council as soon as may be."

Kneller started, and I saw his hand fumble for his glass.

"But surely he knows – "

"Oh, yes," said Sully. "He knows that he will not be there. *He wishes you sworn at the first Council held by Duke Paul.*"

What more was said I did not hear, but Kneller's ears were crimson and his hands were very busy behind his back. Indeed, it was very plain that his withers were wrung, for for the rest of the day he never sat down, but constantly paced the corridor, frowning and blowing through his nose and pulling his heavy moustache. I began to have hope that Kneller might be reclaimed.

Little more than half an hour later George came to say that the door of the south antechamber must now be manned and that young Grimm must mind the back door, because the sergeant-footman had been called to the Prince.

Argument was not to be thought of, but the hall might have been a scaffold upon which we three poor wretches were going to strut.

Two minutes later Bell had taken my place, George was at the door from the staircase, and I stood to that of the antechamber, salver in hand.

It was the practice of visitors to present their cards: these the footman accepted and took to the lord-in-waiting, who immediately repaired to the antechamber and spoke with whoever was there.

Thirty-four visitors paid their respects that day.

I do not know why I had not expected Madame Dresden. As the Grand Duchess' lady-in-waiting, she called at the palace daily. I never knew this nor had given the matter a thought, but at half past ten that morning I was looking into her eyes.

The sentries were watching us, and I was greatly afraid that either she or I had shown some sign of surprise, and, to tell the truth, I can remember no more until I heard her greet Kneller and ask for news.

It was approaching midday when I heard a sound in the antechamber which even the massive mahogany could not shut out – the sharp smack and jingle of heavy spurred heels.

The sentries had sprung to attention.

Now they had not saluted Kneller, and though several officers had called, they had paid them no compliments. This, no doubt, was in order, for the men's manner was very punctilious and, so far as I had seen, they never moved a muscle, but only their eyes.

For an instant my brain faltered. Then the truth leaped into my mind.

It was the Duke Johann.

There is a Latin saying that those whom God will destroy He first sends mad. Dully I acknowledged the truth of the saw. That we had not foreseen that Johann would present himself argued that George and I were out of our minds.

Instead of watching the telltale, I looked round helplessly.

George Hanbury's door was open. He seemed to be receiving some message from someone without. Bell was watching him closely, ready, no doubt, to go for one of the Grimms. Of the two, George was the nearest, and he was twenty paces away. The lord-in-waiting was staring out of the window six paces from where I stood.

I made a frantic effort to marshal my wits.

For Johann to set eyes upon me was clearly dangerous. He would not know me from Adam, but he might very well know that Grimm had dismissed three footmen the night before. And if he knew young Grimm by sight… Again, the Duke Johann had need of no visiting card. I should have to announce his presence – and I dared not trust my voice.

Suddenly I remembered the telltale.

This was dull, but I had no means of knowing whether it had lighted or no.

I dropped my salver.

When I had picked it up, I saw that the telltale was glowing – to my disordered mind as never before.

Kneller had turned and was staring. He was clearly a martinet. A footman's salver to him was the trooper's sword.

There was nothing for it – I went up to Kneller and bowed.

"My lord," I mumbled, "will speak with the Duke Johann?"

God knows what he thought of my accent, but my voice was husky with emotion, and maybe that covered it up.

In any event he followed me back to the door, and I swung this open directly and shut it as soon as I dared.

His manner was so hostile that I made sure that on returning he would take me to task, but I think that his speech with Johann put my failings out of his mind, for when he re-entered the hall he did not seem to see me, and, very soon after, Brooch came to his relief and he went away.

One ordeal we were spared, and that was a visit from Duke Paul. As I have said, he had the right of entry into the hall itself: but though he had been in the habit of coming to inquire for his great-uncle, if not of visiting the Prince, Sully had stopped these visits when Johann took command of the Body Guard. Again by Sully's advice, the Grand Duchess stayed away: and though she had a lady-in-waiting who could come in her stead, no male of the royal house, except the Prince, was accorded the honour of a regular equerry.

For the next three hours our hands were not quite so full, but we had no sort of respite, and even the wretched meal we tried to make was so much interrupted that at last we cared not whether we ate or no.

Here let me say that the Prince's sickness was accounting for this grievous load of duty, which I think twelve footmen could have conveniently shared. When he was well, the Prince, who was vigorous, was out of the palace for the greater part of his day, so that four footmen, although occasionally pressed, had, in the ordinary way, leisure to spare.

Kneller returned to duty at three o'clock – to my inquietude, for, compared with him, Brooch was benevolence itself. The latter's eyes and ears were none too keen, and the one or two orders he gave me were pleasantly given and easy enough to fulfil. What was more, he spent his time reading, but, as I have said, Kneller was very restless and never sat down. Indeed, if Bell had known German, I should have done my best to keep out of Kneller's sight; for I knew he had not forgiven me for letting fall my salver or for bungling my announcement of the presence of Duke Johann, and so was on the look-out for any misconduct of mine upon which he could pounce. The best we could contrive, however, was that I should man the door from the staircase and Hanbury that of the bedchamber, for if the lord-in-waiting had any commands, he was not likely to call the janitor. Bell was to watch the back door, and the Grimms, so far as they could, would stay at the end of the hall, for from there they could see us all three and so could instantly respond to any signal of distress.

It was about four o'clock that I opened my door some six inches to see before me the man that I had hit in the stomach on the day that we came to Barabbas against our will.

That there might be no doubt about it, he had a card in his hand, and, when I presented a salver, I saw that the card bore the name of Martin Egge.

He gave me no sign of recognition: but be sure I lost no time in shutting the door.

At once I looked for assistance, and the sergeant-footman stepped to my side.

"I know this man," I whispered. "He must not see me again."

"Very well," said he, and took the card to Kneller, who was pacing the hall.

When Kneller had read the name he showed signs of concern. I fancy he knew Martin Egge for a creature of Duke Johann's, and did not wish to see him, yet could not bring himself to send him away.

At length –

"Desire him to wait," he said.

Grimm returned to the door and requested the fellow to wait in the south antechamber.

"I cannot wait," said the other. "I must either be admitted or go."

"I may not admit you, sir. It is against the rule."

The visitor shrugged his shoulders and stood where he was.

As I shut the door –

"What does he say?" growled Kneller, three paces away.

"That he cannot wait, my lord," said Grimm. "He must either be admitted or go."

Kneller grew red in the face.

Then –

"I will go out," he said thickly.

I opened the door to the staircase, and Kneller passed out.

I looked at the sergeant-footman, who was frowning upon the door.

"Listen," said I. "He should not have left the suite."

"No," said Grimm. "He should not."

"You take the door," said I. "That was one of Duke Johann's men."

Before he could reply I was gone, and had signed to George to follow me out of sight.

I cannot think how I smelled danger, but the sight of Egge had shocked me, and his inconvenient persistence had seemed to me something deliberate, and not the instance of a man who has truly no time to spare. I felt that he had wished to lure Kneller out of the suite.

Be that as it may, as the sergeant-footman stood to the door, every moment expecting his son to take Hanbury's place, he saw Johann enter the hall from the south antechamber.

Exactly what passed between them I never knew, but though Grimm showed the man out, he was clearly badly shaken by the line which Johann had taken and his menacing air.

This much I learned.

Johann had justified his entry by declaring that he had been 'ringing' for several minutes, in vain and then had said that, *now that Grimm was short-handed*, he had better have three or four sentries to keep the doors.

Grimm had replied that he would take the Prince's pleasure upon that point.

Johann had then asked where was the lord-in-waiting, and Grimm had been forced to admit that he was not in the suite.

Upon this Johann had said that if the lords-in-waiting and servants were not at their posts, he would have to consider his position and whether it was not his duty to man the apartments himself.

With that he took himself off, having had, to my mind, very much the best of the round, for, though he was clean out of order, he had caught Kneller napping and Grimm alone in the hall: he had proved 'the nakedness of the land', and, if now he determined to relieve it, I did not see that his proposal could be reasonably condemned.

As the door closed upon him, young Grimm, who had been detained, arrived at the door to the stairs, and an instant later Kneller re-entered the hall. By the grace of God, therefore, Johann and the lord-in-waiting did not meet, and the former was spared the knowledge that there were in fact four footmen as heretofore. But the keeping of this secret seemed like to cost us as dear as its revelation, and it was desperately clear that any moment now the ice upon which we were treading was going to crack.

Before, however, we could even discuss this very serious turn, the Prince was calling for Grimm, and while the latter was with him, the Court clockmaker came to wind the clocks. While he was about his business, two prelates arrived, and, the Prince's pleasure being learned, were ushered into his chamber to comfort their sovereign lord. By the time the two were gone it was half past four, and from then until half past five, representatives of foreign Courts came to the antechamber to pay their respects.

After six o'clock the calls upon our activity diminished to some extent, but though we tried more than once to hold a hasty council and have at the matter with Grimm, each time we were interrupted almost before we had begun and at last we saw that it was hopeless and abandoned the attempt.

Indeed, I shall never know how Grimm and his son were able to cope with the duty at this time the day before: but young

Grimm declared that the calls had been much less frequent and that the Prince had been dozing and so had not sent for his father for nearly two hours.

At five minutes to nine that evening I ushered the doctors out of the royal apartments, and two or three minutes later Brooch took his leave for the night.

I shut the door behind him, sank down on the bench beside me and buried my face in my hands.

To make use of a slang expression, I was all in.

At half past two the next morning somebody touched my arm.

Dead asleep as I had been, I was wide awake in an instant, after the way of the soldier that is holding some hopeless lodgment and has his being in constant dread of attack.

George Hanbury and Grimm were beside me.

"There's a change in the Prince's condition," said George quickly. "It's slight, but eloquent. The nuns are perfectly persuaded that this is the end."

"Have they rung for the doctors?"

"Not yet. They don't propose to until there is more to be seen. The doctors, they say, would probably laugh them to scorn."

"How long do they give him?" said I.

"They won't be tied down," said George. "But, so far as I can gather, from three to six hours."

I got to my feet.

"We must press for the minimum," said I. I turned to Grimm. "Will you go and ask them if they would be astonished if the Prince were dead in an hour? Put it like that."

He nodded and disappeared, and I went to drink some water and bathe my face.

As I returned, he emerged from the Prince's room.

"The Prince will live for an hour, sir – most likely for two or three. He may live for six or seven hours: but that he should die under the hour they will not have."

"Very well," said I: "then Rowley must leave at once."

As I had half expected, the sergeant-footman demurred.

It would, he maintained, be most awkward for her Highness and Duke Paul and Sully to be waiting in the private apartments for five or six hours: there was no fit accommodation: once there, they would be his charge, and take so much upon him he could not at such a time.

"Listen," said I. "There's a risk of their coming too early, and a risk of their coming too late. We cannot take the second, and so we must take the first."

George supported me stoutly, and at length the old servant gave way.

We opened the door to the passage and sent Rowley off.

"And now," said I, "to business. Bringing them in is nothing. We've got to tie up Johann."

For the next thirty minutes we hammered and beat upon this problem, as a smith upon the red-hot iron.

The doctors must presently be summoned, and so must Kneller and Brooch. Johann might have to be summoned, or he might not. Grimm had not summoned him before – the fellow had simply appeared. Whether a doctor had warned him, or one of the lords-in-waiting, neither Grimm nor his son could tell. It might have been one of the footmen that Grimm had dismissed. This, of course, was the devil. The last thing we wanted was Johann *before his time*.

One thing was clear as daylight – once it was known that the heir apparent's adherents were in the private apartments, *no one, but one of us five, must leave the suite*.

Without a doubt, Johann had issued his orders a week ago – orders to be carried out the moment he gave the word. They might or might not be sealed – most likely they were. But that his Adjutant had them I was perfectly sure. And at a word from Johann he would instantly set to work to carry them out.

That word must never be given – must never be sent.

There were within call eight sentries – eight men-at-arms. Once he was in the suite, their Colonel-in-Chief had only to raise his voice for them to enter the apartments and come to his side.

That voice must never be raised.

What harassed us to distraction was how to deal with Johann.

We dreaded his presence: yet we dared not leave him at large. If he did not come, he must be summoned, and then – what then?

Sandbag the man we dared not. For one thing only, the Body Guard was under his orders and would surely wait upon these. For another, neither Sully nor Kneller would countenance such an act. Johann was of royal blood.

Let me put it like this.

A pretender to the throne, Johann had to be crushed: as a duke of the royal house, he had to be spared: but, as commanding the Body Guard, *he had to be used.*

The Body Guard held the palace. All the goings and comings, consequent upon the death of the sovereign, would be under their hand: they would provide, or withhold, the orderlies, escorts and guards which a due observance of the passing of the throne would require: except by their leave, the people of Riechtenburg could not be so much as informed of the death of the Prince.

Even if Kneller stayed faithful, I found it hard to believe that the Second-in-command of the Body Guard would take the General's orders, unless they came through Johann.

"Deadlock," said George, in the end. "I can't see any way out. If we all look ugly enough, he may find it rather awkward to call the guard: but we can't order them off and, if we do, I don't imagine they'll go. His game is to smile – *and wait.* Sully produces Duke Paul and says 'Here's the king.' 'Right-o,' says Johann. '*You play him.*' And, if he says that, Sully's stuck. He damned well can't play his king. For one thing, he's out of touch. Post-office, press and public are out of his reach. Even the telephone's gone. But Johann's not out of touch…

Here the door of the wardrobe was opened and Sully stepped out.

I shall never forget his coming.

Instead of the agitation which I had made sure he would show, he was as calm and unruffled as I had ever seen him, and his cool, dignified bearing and the steady look in his eyes put me to shame.

Before we could speak, he set his hands upon our shoulders and lowered his head.

"If I were married," he said, "I should pray that my sons might have your courage, your wit, and your address – and I should pray in vain. If I had not seen it myself, I would not have believed that the spirit could so dominate the flesh."

'Courage and address.' Had he seen me when I dropped my salver, I fancy that he would have chosen less shining words.

"Don't believe it now," said George. "We're a couple of broken reeds."

Sully smiled.

"I have learned of you," he said. "You have given me confidence: and nothing that you can say can take it away."

"I'm thankful for that," said I, and began to examine the problem which George and I could not solve.

To my surprise he stopped me.

"If we had six months," he said, "we could preconceive no plan. We must deal with what happens when it happens, as best we may."

"I think," said I, "that you may need our support."

"I depend upon it," said Sully. "I know that you will do nothing rash, and of that knowledge I shall question nothing that you do."

With his words, Grimm came out of the bedchamber. In his eyes was the look of distress you may see in the eyes of a dog.

"The Prince is worse, sirs," he said. "I think that the doctors should be summoned. He – he does not know me."

George and I looked at one another.

"If we summon the doctors," said I, "we must summon the lords-in-waiting. And that may mean that we are summoning Johann."

"Let it be done," said Sully. "We must ourselves be in order at any cost."

A bell in the Prince's study would summon the lords-in-waiting. Grimm told his son to ring this and then to man the door from the staircase instead of Bell. Bell would man that of the bedchamber.

I entered the wardrobe and, kneeling by the door from the passage, strained my ears.

I could hear nothing.

It was now nearly forty minutes since Rowley had gone.

I returned to Sully.

"Do you know," I asked him, "whether they have a car?"

"Yes," said he. "In case that of Madame Dresden was not ready, I sent mine to the Duke's lodging and came here on foot."

There was nothing to be said.

Within five minutes I heard the doctors arrive.

A moment later Grimm came out of the room.

"The Prince is sinking, sirs. He will not live for two hours. When they said that, I asked the doctors to tell me when I should summon the chaplain and Duke Johann. They promised to give me the word."

"Well done," said I.

"But I think the Duke Johann may come, sir, without we send. My lord Brooch may give him the word."

"So do I," said I. "For that reason Bell must come in, and you and your son alone must appear in the hall. If Duke Johann comes, is there any reason why he should not be put in the dining-room?"

"Between that and the bedchamber, sir, there is a connecting door."

"I know," said I. "Put him into the dining-room. He won't demur. If he does – *it's the Prince's pleasure*. We must keep him as far from the sentries as ever we can."

"I'm in your hands, sir," said Grimm.

With that, he went off, and I returned to the wardrobe, where George and Sully were standing by the side of the open trap.

I raised my eyebrows, and Hanbury shook his head.

Rowley had been gone fifty minutes – to be exact, fifty-two.

Bell came to say that the lords-in-waiting had arrived. The sergeant-footman had met them and made his report.

I could not stand still waiting, but went after Grimm. He was, of course, in the hall.

"Tell me," I whispered. "If Duke Johann has to be summoned, whom will you send?"

"I have thought of that, sir. One of the holy women can seek the chaplain and she can tell one of the servants to fetch the Duke. And now will you take my place? I should be in the bedchamber."

I did not know what to do.

The man was quite right. His place was in the sick-room. More. Unless he was in the sick-room, we had no means of knowing the state of the Prince. Yet, in case Johann should arrive, he must be in the hall.

"Listen," said I. "I will send Bell to stand here – by the bedchamber door. You also will stand by the door – but *inside* the room. The instant a telltale glows Bell will knock twice. Then he will disappear and you will enter the hall."

"Very well, sir."

By the time the change had been made, another five minutes had passed.

George was on the floor of the wardrobe, with his head overhanging the opening, straining his ears. Sully was standing beside him, leaning against the door of one of the several closets which gave the wardrobe its name. As the latter's eyes met mine, the wise smile I had seen so often came into his face.

A wave of admiration swept into my heart.

The weight upon Sully's shoulders was far more heavy than any we sought to bear. The master he loved lay dying: everything that he cared for was in the scale: this hole and corner business was as strange and odious to his nature as is the sunlight to the owl. Yet of us all he was the calmest, the most assured.

I saw George thrust down his head.

For a moment he listened intently. Then he nodded and rose to his knees.

"They're coming," he breathed. "I can hear them. In half a minute you'll see the light of the torch."

"Praise God," said I, and meant it, and Sully's lips moved as though he had said 'Amen'.

It was now exactly an hour since Rowley had been dispatched.

As I stood to the top of the steps, I heard a double knock fall upon the bedchamber's door...

The footfalls were clear now.

The three were hastening – almost running. As luck would have it, the floor of the passage was smooth, and indeed the whole of the tunnel was very well done.

The Grand Duchess was mounting the steps.

She had jewels in her hair, and a cloak of gold and crimson overlaid the black of her dress.

Her face was most white and set, and when she saw me, she instantly looked elsewhere, as though to avoid my eyes.

Wondering, I put out an arm, for the steps were high; but, though she lowered her head, as though to acknowledge the gesture, she made no use of my help.

I moved to one side – dazedly.

As she stepped into the wardrobe she covered her eyes.

I glanced at the Countess Dresden, behind on the steps. In her face was plain tragedy.

186

I returned to the Grand Duchess, to see that her mouth was working against her will.

"What is it?" I breathed. "What's the matter?"

Twice she strove to answer, but no words came.

Then she drew herself up.

"Gentlemen," she said, "it is finished. *Duke Paul – the heir is not with us. I am here to tell you, to my shame, that he is afraid to come.*"

The silence which succeeded her words was that of death. Sully, George and I stood as though turned to stone. And the Grand Duchess stood in our midst, like some Andromache, stricken, desperate and – incomparable.

The sergeant-footman entered the wardrobe and came to my side.

Though I heard what he said, he seemed to me to be speaking from a great way off.

"Sir," he whispered, "I have done as you said. His Highness the Duke Johann is in the dining-room."

9

We Play the King

I suppose there have been moments in history when a king himself has cast his kingdom away, but I find it hard to believe that, since the world began rolling, anyone having authority, high or low, has ever failed his supporters so untimely and so outright.

I had always feared that, if he were summoned by night, Duke Paul would take his own time to leave his bed and might imperil his fortune by his delay; but I had never dreamed that, bidden to his own accession, he would refuse to come.

Indeed, the Grand Duchess' tidings acted upon me as some malignant drug. I felt as though I had suffered a blow on the head which had not laid me senseless, but had disabled my wits. These lay dormant. I could see and hear: I could smell the faint perfume which the Grand Duchess used. But use my brain I could not: that member was stunned.

I regarded Grimm stupidly: I surveyed the Countess Dresden as though I had not seen her before: and I stared upon the Grand Duchess as a clown upon some beautiful waxwork which represents a kind of which he has never dreamed.

Then I saw George turn to Sully, and my presence of mind came back.

"I will go," I said, and hardly knew my own voice. "The Prince must not die – *officially*, before I return." I looked at George. "If the doctors can't see our point, man the bedroom and show them something they can."

The next moment I was in the passage, with Rowley running before me as hard as he could.

What was the length of the tunnel I do not know, but at that time it seemed to be endless, and at last, of my impatience, I overtook Rowley and snatched the torch from his hand.

As we left the niche, I saw that night was still with us and would be for half an hour, but the sky was not so black as it is at midnight, and I knew that the dawn was coming over the hills.

I had hoped against hope to find a car by the fosse, but when I asked Rowley he told me that the Grand Duchess had alighted a little way off and, before going on, had sent the chauffeur away.

There was nothing for it but to run as fast as we could.

Our course lay by the river and in front of the palace gates, but the breadth of the road would lie between us and the sentries, and, though the light of the lamps might show my livery, the men were not likely to take action, and, in any event, Rowley knew no other way.

I am not fleet of foot, and before we had covered five furlongs I was in some distress; but I dared not spare myself, for I knew it was neck or nothing – and a very close run.

By the time we had passed the palace I was streaming with sweat and my lungs were beginning to labour as never before; then a stitch came to torment me and my legs started trembling and aching from ankle to hip: but any torture was better than the horror of losing time, and I stumbled on like a madman, with Rowley panting behind.

All the time despair possessed me. My aim was to fetch Duke Paul, but how to bring this about I could not think. That the Duke would hear me of all men seemed out of reason: as like as not he would have me turned from his doors. Even if he yielded to persuasion, he never would hasten as we had, and I could not command a car. Meanwhile the Prince was *in extremis*, and I had set George Hanbury an almost impossible task.

At last Rowley spurted past me and turned to the left. This to guide me, for we were past speaking, and but for his movement I should have run straight on.

If we passed anyone I did not see them: but that is nothing to go by, for even my sight was failing beneath the strain. The ways seemed less dark than blurred, and the trees upon either side to be closing in. I could not hear our footfalls, but only a dull roaring, like that of the waves of the sea; and I blundered rather than ran, for all my steps were uncertain, and the merest wrinkle in the roadway troubled my balance and threw me out of my stride.

Rowley lurched to the right, and we entered a broad street which seemed familiar, to see in the distance the lights of a car standing to the left of the way.

I tried to cry out, but I could not, so I made a mighty effort to reach Rowley's side. As I came abreast, I touched him: then I staggered on to the pavement and, seizing the railing of a mansion, hung upon it like a wretch on a whipping-post, to get my breath. If I was to argue, it was clear I must be able to speak.

So for two precious minutes we let the world slip.

Then we went halting together up to the car.

As I had prayed, this was Sully's.

I told the chauffeur that the Duke would be out in a moment, and, after staring a little, he touched his hat.

I bade Rowley stand by the car and rang the house-bell.

The mansion was not in darkness, and almost at once a butler opened the door.

"His Highness Duke Paul," I demanded, "in the name of the Prince."

Before he could answer I was within the house.

Now I was far from recovered and was breathing most hard, and I fancy I had the look of a desperate man. If my speech was strange, I was wearing the royal livery, and the servants were doubtless aware, if not that the Prince was dying, that some state crisis was at hand.

Be that as it may, the butler left the door open and ran before me upstairs and into a smoking-room.

As we entered the chamber, I heard the shiver of glass.

Duke Paul was in the midst of the floor, unusually red in the face and regarding the pane of a china-cupboard from which was protruding the hassock which he had launched. He was wearing the gay uniform in which I had seen him last.

He stared at me as though I were risen from the dead.

"Leave us," said I to the butler.

The fellow went.

I turned to the Duke.

"My lord," said I, "have no fear. If you come with me, in an hour you will be the Prince."

He began to pluck at his lip.

"I – I thought you – "

"I know. You thought I had been arrested for something I hadn't done." He recoiled. "Never mind. This isn't vengeance. I'm about the only person with whom you're really safe. And now please come with me. There's a car below."

The youth's eyes narrowed.

"Come with you?" he snarled. "I've a good mind to – And why are you wearing those things? You're an impostor, a — traitor. That's what you are. And I know what your game is – you can't fool me."

"My game doesn't matter," said I. "The point is I'm out to save yours. I've come from the sergeant-footman – from Grimm. The Prince is *in extremis*, and I've been sent to fetch you as quick as I can."

The Duke was convulsed with a mirth which was rather too forced to be true.

"Oh, my aunt," he said slowly. "Forgive me, but I guess you don't know. Royalty aren't fetched by footmen. An ADC, or an equerry – "

"Grieg, for instance," said I.

He started at that. Then he pointed to the door.

"Get out of this," he said. "If you don't, I'll send for the police. If I was wanted at the palace, they would have telephoned."

"The wires have been cut."

"Then Sully would have come and – "

"His car's outside," said I.

The fellow stamped his foot.

"Don't argue," he raved. "Get out. I tell you I know your game. You're an adventurer – that's what you are. Trying to worm yourself in. A common adventurer. If you aren't, why didn't you go? Why have you hung about here? Why – "

My temper was rising, but I strove to keep it in hand.

"Listen," said I. "Sully's an old friend of mine, and I'm trying to help him to – "

"It's a lie," yelled the Duke. "It's nothing to do with Sully. *You're Leonie's lover, you are.* And this a plot between you, to get me out of the way."

In a flash I had moved and had the man by the throat.

"By rights I should choke you," I said. "Instead of that, I'm going to save your throne." I drew my pistol and put it up to his face. "We are going downstairs and into the car outside. I shall hold this pistol under the tail of my coat. If you call upon your servants or try to bolt, as sure as I live I'll fire." I let him go and stood back. "Take up your hat and come."

He was pale as death now, and without so much as a murmur he did as I said.

"I shall be behind you," said I, "with my eyes on your back."

He opened the door and passed out and down the stairs.

The butler saw us coming and opened the door of the house.

In the hall the Duke wavered.

"Go on," said I, grimly.

He passed out and into the car.

Then Rowley took his seat by the chauffeur and we drove for the fosse…

Not another word passed between us until we were treading the passage in single file.

Halfway along I called upon Rowley to stop. Then I addressed the Duke.

"In a moment," said I, "we shall be in the Prince's wardrobe. The Prince is dying, or dead, so you will make no noise. Sully is there waiting. Presently Duke Johann will appear. We shall see that he does you no harm, *so long as you hold your tongue*. Whatever he says, hold your tongue and let Sully play the hand. If you don't do this, if you don't take your cue from Sully – in a word, if you play the fool, Johann can wring your neck, and I'll stand by and watch him do it, with my hands on my hips."

With that, I bade Rowley lead on, and two minutes later I saw the light from the wardrobe shining down on to the steps.

Bell was down on a knee by the side of the trap.

As the Duke passed into the wardrobe –

"Is the Prince alive?" I whispered.

"I've no idea, sir. Mr Hanbury's in the bedroom, holding the door to the hall, and we were to go in at once the moment you came."

For the fiftieth time that morning I wiped my face.

I never saw livery yet that was fit to run in, and though all the world has heard of 'a running footman', I fancy such men were in training and specially clad. There was no time to change my linen, but, when I asked him, Bell declared this would pass, and I can only hope that I did not look the sloven I felt.

As Bell was dusting my slippers, I heard the Grand Duchess' voice.

"Sully is in the bedroom. Mr Hanbury wants you to enter and stand to the dining-room door."

An instant later we were within the room.

From my place by the dining-room door I regarded the memorable scene.

The chamber was large but very simply furnished, and, except for a great pier-glass, the walls were bare. Heavy crimson curtains tempered the fresh night air, but the windows behind them were full open, and the room was agreeably cool.

On the smallest four-post bed I have ever seen lay the dying Prince.

He was raised so high with pillows that the bedclothes came but to his waist, and a white shawl of Shetland wool had been tucked about his body to take their place. His eyes were shut, and he lay as still as the marble to which he was soon to go. I could not have told if he was living, but that a doctor beside him had fingers about his wrist: yet, had I not known that he was dying, I doubt that it would have entered my head. The sting of death, the victory of the grave were not to be thought of: on the proud old face was a look which denied such old wives' tales: calm, careless, infinitely content, it made death seem a slight business, more like the listening to music than the leaving of life.

On his knees by the bed was the chaplain, and the nuns were kneeling behind him with lowered heads. At the head of the bed stood the doctors, one upon either side, and beside them stood Sully and Grimm, ready to catch any murmur from the lips of the man they served.

At the foot of the bed was Duke Paul, unearthly pale and standing stiffly at attention with his eyes on his great-uncle's face. To his left the Grand Duchess was kneeling, with Madame Dresden behind. And that was all – save for the three state footmen standing before the doors.

The physicians exchanged a glance. Then one leaned towards Sully and spoke in his ear. For a moment they whispered together. Then Sully turned to Grimm.

At once the sergeant-footman stole to my side.

"The Lord Sully, sir, has told me to summon the Duke Johann." He hesitated. "When – when it is over, please to set this door open and then yourself go directly into the dining-room. Mr Hanbury wants you to man the door to the hall."

I nodded. Then I stood aside and opened my door...

Johann came in delicately, with Kneller and Brooch behind. He took, I think, two paces. Then he started violently and stopped in his tracks.

There were four of us penned behind him, but the man never moved.

Unable to shut my door, I watched him curiously.

I have seen men taken aback, but I have never seen anyone so manifestly confounded or so very plainly reluctant to believe his own eyes: and I must confess to a fleeting sense of triumph and the thought that, could he have seen it, Prince Nicholas would have relished the knave's discomfiture.

For a little he gazed at Duke Paul: then he looked at Sully, and a hand went up to his head. Suddenly he noticed George Hanbury, and I saw his shock of surprise: from him he glanced to Bell, and then swung about sharply to stare upon me.

His movements were hardly human – rather were they those of a puppet which is jerked to and fro: and I think he would have stood gazing for two minutes or more, if Grimm had not made to pass by to come to the bed.

As a man in a dream, he gave way, and, when Kneller and Grimm had moved on, I shut the door.

Brooch stood where he was, by Johann: he was plainly badly shaken, for he kept his eyes fast upon the carpet, and I saw his grey head wagging against his will.

Johann seemed to collect himself and glanced at the Prince. Then he folded his arms and lowered his head.

Five long minutes went by.

Then Nicholas, Prince of Riechtenberg, lifted a hand to his chin.

For a moment his fingers strayed. Then his brows drew into a frown.

"Grimm, where's the barber?" he said.

I saw his old servant start forward, as a dog that is named, but there was no mind behind the question, and before he could make any answer the frown was gone.

The fingers left the chin and sank to the breast...

Another two minutes stole by.

Then very gently the doctor let go the wrist he had held so long.

"Gentlemen," he said, "it is over. His Royal Highness is dead."

For a long moment nobody moved.

Then I turned on my heel and opened my door.

I set it wide and passed through – to the door which led out of the dining-room into the hall.

There I took my stand, with my back to the mahogany and, if I am to be honest, with my heart in my mouth.

Duke Paul entered the room, white as a sheet. I could see his eyes shifting to and fro, as though he would see behind him without turning his head.

At his heels came the Grand Duchess, a little paler than usual, but very calm.

I saw her glance over her shoulder. Then she touched the Duke's arm and pointed to a massive armchair. He took his seat there, and she passed to his left.

Johann entered slowly, and I saw his eyes fly to the door before which I stood. He put the table between himself and Duke Paul.

Sully followed and moved to the right of Duke Paul.

The Countess Dresden stepped to the Grand Duchess' side.

The lords-in-waiting entered – Kneller, dark red in the face, and Brooch, the colour of parchment, moistening his lips.

Last of all came George Hanbury, and shut the door.

The Lord President looked about him and folded his hands. Then he lifted his voice.

"His Royal Highness," said Sully, "will hold a Council this morning at ten o'clock. There are certain matters, however, which may not so long be left, which fall to be dealt with by the Lord President, aided by such of the Household as he may call upon. These are the tolling of the great bell of St Jude's, the discharge of the minute guns, the issue of summonses and the *communiqué*: finally there is the Proclamation of Prince Paul which must in accordance with custom be made in the forecourt of the palace at nine o'clock."

He paused there, and Johann cleared his throat.

"My presence is not needed," he said, and turned to the door.

"Your Highness," said Sully quietly, "will be pleased to remain. It is the Prince's pleasure."

Johann turned.

"I will return," he said shortly. "As commanding the Body Guard, I have orders to give."

Again he turned to the door.

"Your Highness," said Sully coldly, "misunderstood what I said. The Prince desires your presence."

Johann hesitated. Then he shrugged his shoulders and turned.

"Well?" he said sharply.

"The Proclamation," said Sully, "depends upon the – "

"Is it customary," said Johann, "that during the private discussion of matters of State, servants should remain in the room?"

"It is the Prince's pleasure."

Johann drew himself up.

"My Lord President," he said, "since we have been in this room Duke Paul has not opened his mouth. When I wish to go about my business, it is you that command me to stay: when I protest that the servants should leave the room, it is you that quash my remonstrance out of hand. You take too much upon you, my lord. I do not allow that such conduct is convenient or customary."

"Your Highness," said Sully, "will appreciate that the Prince can hardly be expected to be familiar with the discharge of an office to which he succeeded only five minutes ago."

"He has a tongue," said Johann.

"I am his spokesman," said Sully. "If I go too far for his liking, his Royal Highness will pull me up. Till then, it is my bounden duty – "

"Why your duty?"

"By virtue of my office," said Sully.

"I take precedence of you."

"Without doubt, sir," said Sully. "But you are not an Officer of State."

"I command the Body Guard."

"What of that, sir? Since when has the Colonel of the Guard advised his Sovereign?"

Johann made a gesture of impatience.

"I dispute," he said, "your right to assume the functions of Prince."

There was a little silence.

Then –

"Why do you?" said the Grand Duchess. "I don't."

Johann's eyes narrowed.

"Madam," he said darkly, "I counsel you to keep your hand out of this."

"Out of what?" said the Grand Duchess.

Johann swallowed.

"Out of this difference," he said.

"Why?"

Johann made no answer, but looked very black. As he turned again to Sully –

"You protest," said the Grand Duchess, "that the Lord President is exceeding his authority."

"I do," said Johann.

"What of the Colonel of the Guard?"

Johann started.

"What of him, madam?" he said.

"This. Twenty minutes ago his sentries refused to let me pass. The officer on duty told me that those were your orders."

Johann raised his eyebrows, but I saw his fingers twitching behind his back.

"Then how are you here, madam?"

The Grand Duchess shrugged her shoulders.

"I asked the officer whether he was for you or for Duke Paul."

Slowly the blood came into Johann's face. All eyes were upon him, but his were fast upon the table which stood between him and Duke Paul. He made no attempt to answer, and I fancy his thoughts were unruly and were fighting between themselves.

My lady's downright speech had disconcerted him, but its burden had shaken him badly for all to see. He had no choice but to believe her story – the only explanation of how she had reached the suite. And if the Guard was to fail him…

The man turned to the door and came up to me.

I never moved.

"Open," he said thickly.

I looked him full in the eyes and gave no sign.

For a moment he stood, glowering. Then he swung round.

"So I am prisoner," he said, and let out a laugh.

I saw his hand flash to his breast and take hold of a chain. As he drew the whistle, I took it out of his hand. Then I put up my other hand, snapped the chain asunder and put the whistle away.

"Your Highness," said I, "I have orders that you are to make no noise. I am prepared to go all lengths to carry those orders out. All lengths."

Johann's eyes burned in his head.

At length –

"Who is this man?" he said.

"Ask Grieg," said the Grand Duchess.

I have never seen rage so dominant yet suppressed, and I thought the fellow would have fallen down in a fit. His face was twisted with wrath and his upper lip was lifted like that of a snarling dog.

Presently he turned to the table.

"Your Highness," said Sully firmly, "the murder is out. Everyone in this room is aware of your purpose to make yourself Prince."

There was a long silence, breathless and pregnant.

Brooch looked ready to drop: Kneller stood like a statue, staring ahead.

Johann drew himself up. Then he threw back his head and laughed.

"I reserve my defence," he said shortly. With that, he sat down in a chair and crossed his legs. "There were certain formalities, you were saying. No doubt you will carry them out. The bell to be tolled, for instance, and the minute guns."

There was another silence, and, to be perfectly honest, my heart sank down like a stone.

The worst had happened. Johann had drawn our trumps and was now going to smile – and *wait*. We had come to a deadlock. George Hanbury's prophecy had come true.

Sully's eyes sought mine – desperately: but I had no comfort to give. When I glanced at George, his face was the picture of distress. The Grand Duchess was looking before her, with a little hand to her head.

If proof were needed of our helplessness, it was written in Johann's face. With his last words, his anger seemed to have died, to be succeeded by a confident scorn, far more offensive than his wrath. As though to point his outlook, the fellow stared placidly upon the ceiling and, putting his hands together, began to twiddle his thumbs.

It has been said that the hour will produce the man. Whether that is true, of this case I cannot say, but I am inclined to think that Johann cut his own throat. His insufferable behaviour was too much for an old martinet.

Kneller stepped forward.

Be sure he wasted no words.

"My Lord Duke," he said bluntly, "but one Prince sits at a time, and, unless and until you displace him, you must up on your feet."

Johann drew in his breath.

"So," he said hoarsely. "I thought – "

"So did I, sir," said Kneller. "But, now that I am put to the touch – well, no man can serve two masters, and I am no exception to the rule."

"I shall remember this, Kneller."

"So be it, Lord Duke," rasped the General. "*I am for Prince Paul.* You will please to give me your sword."

Johann rose, glaring.

"Why?"

"For what I have seen, sir, – no more. You have flouted authority: you have trampled good order and discipline under foot. That was uncalled for – and you are the Colonel of the Guard."

Kneller was growing angry, and Johann made another mistake.

"General," he said soothingly, "you forget – "

"Your sword, sir," barked Kneller. "I have put you under arrest."

The fellow made no movement, so I stepped to his side and made to take his sword from its frog.

He raised his hand to strike me, but Hanbury had moved when I had and caught his arm.

I took his sword and scabbard and presented them to the General. He pointed to the table, and I laid them down on the oak.

"And now," said Kneller, "for these Orders." He turned to Duke Paul. "By your Royal Highness' leave, I will send for pen and paper, and the Lord President will tell me what he requires to be done."

The rough draft of those 'Orders to the Body Guard' lies before me today.

It is too long to set out, for it covers two pages of foolscap, and, even if it were shorter, it is but dry matter, bristling with military terms. But I shall always value it, for, by Sully's express desire, George and I suggested certain additions to what Kneller and he had composed, and, though the former grunted and blew through his nose, he shaped them to our joint liking and then embodied them without a word.

Then he made a fair copy, and Johann signed his name at the foot of the sheet – this at the point of my pistol and after an ugly scene. For all that, he did it, and Kneller took the Orders to the Orderly Room before the ink was dry.

Ten minutes later the sentries were withdrawn from the doors of the private apartments. By that time the telephone was working, and the Second-in-command of the Body Guard reported in person to Kneller at five o'clock.

Perhaps because it was Sunday, all Vigil came thronging to hear the Proclamation at nine o'clock.

Five minutes before the hour I opened the great French window at the end of the hall, and George and I stepped on to the balcony.

At the sight of the state liveries a long murmur of excitement came from the crowds. These were without the forecourt. The broad boulevard between the gates and the river was choked with a press of people which stretched far beyond the palace on either side. To the right, the Bridge of Arches was lodging a multitude through which no traffic could have passed, and even across the water I could see the embankment swarming and the windows of the houses alive with citizens.

In the forecourt itself two squadrons of the Black Hussars were mounting guard – one in column and the other lining the enclosure from end to end. Before and below the balcony the trumpeters sat in their saddles with their trumpets upon their thighs. A little crowd of privileged persons, most of whom wore some uniform or other, was looking towards the Grand Entrance which lay on its left. This was directly below the balcony and was, therefore, out of my sight, so that, though I heard it, to this day I do not know who made the Proclamation or, indeed, what company stood by his side upon the steps; but that Sully was there with Kneller I have no doubt.

George and I took our stand, one at each end of the balcony, which was some seven feet long.

Looking down, I saw the sergeant-trumpeter watching my face. In the mouth of the window behind me stood Grimm, with his watch in his hand.

So we stood waiting in the hot sunshine, while the river ran white against the piers of the Bridge of Arches and the crowds swayed and whispered and the troop-horses stamped and shivered, to rout the flies.

"Two minutes to the hour, sir," said Grimm. "I am going to fetch the Prince."

It seemed to me an age before he was back.

At last –

"Half a minute to the hour, sir. Will you please count thirty seconds and give the sign?"

I counted thirty. Then I looked at the sergeant-trumpeter and nodded my head.

He gave an order, and the trumpeters raised their arms.

Floating across the water came the agreeable jingle of the Cathedral bells.

Then the long fanfare rang out, and the Prince and the Grand Duchess stepped on to the balcony.

I dared not look at my lady; but she was standing beside me and, since the balcony was small, so close that I could smell her perfume and tell when she bent her head.

What was in her mind at that moment I cannot tell, but I know that I was glad of her presence, for here was the end she had wanted – the consummation she had so desperately wished, and I had done my part to bring it about.

My thoughts flung back to Barabbas and that other sunshiny morning when I had stood by her side – when she had asked me to help her and I had promised to do whatever she asked.

'Once he's proclaimed'…

Duke Johann was not present. I doubt if he heard the cheers. He was seated on the steps of the passage, and the door to the wardrobe was shut. Brooch and Rowley were with him, but I think the man needed no guard. There was no more spirit in him, and, when, later on, he was given the choice of standing his trial by court-martial or resigning his Commission and withdrawing from Riechtenburg, he immediately chose withdrawal and requested permission to leave the palace by the passage under cover of night.

Here let me say that he was the last to use that tunnel which had cost him so dear, for, at my instance, masons were put to work and both of its mouths were sealed the following day.

Prince Paul's servants relieved us at half past nine, and I must confess that I never put off any clothing with so much thankfulness.

Now we would have slipped away by the way we had come, but for the warrant that was running for our arrest. Not that we meant to stay in Vigil, but we wished to visit our flat, to make our toilet and to take away our baggage without any fuss. We had, therefore, to speak with Sully; and, since he was up to his ears in business of State, we had to make up our minds to wait at least until the Council was done. And this was the devil, for now we were fish out of water in very truth, and had nowhere to go or to turn for an hour and a half.

At one end of the hall was all the panoply of Death – flowers and prelates and two dragoons standing with arms reversed; at the other, the bustle of Accession was prevailing, while the servants' quarters were agog with wide-eyed footmen, constantly seeking instruction and very much afraid of Grimm, who was fuming to see a confusion with which he could hardly cope.

We would have withdrawn to the wardrobe, but, when the Proclamation was over, this had been allotted to Johann; and there he and Brooch were sitting, in as gloomy a silence as ever two sinners preserved, waiting till night should come, to go their ways.

At ten o'clock precisely Prince Paul, with Sully and Kneller, left the suite, to go to the Council Chamber a few yards away, and two or three minutes later young Grimm made his way to my side.

"Sir," said he, "the Grand Duchess wishes to see you before she goes."

I followed him to the hall, very conscious of being in the way and of cutting a figure which would have been sent packing from any but the humblest of inns.

My clothes were those that had suffered in my brush with the police. I had no collar, and my shirt was so tattered as scarce to be worth putting on. My coat I had long ago discarded, and, though my overalls did much to cover these shortcomings, I had so faithfully fouled them, that these were not fit to be seen. Add to this that I had not been able to get the powder out of my hair, so that I was more fit to scare crows than to have to do with a lady of high degree.

Yet, at the sight of my lady I forgot my looks.

She came to meet me quickly, with the sweetest smile on her lips.

A few feet away stood the Countess, and, as well as the two men-at-arms, two footmen were in the hall.

"I have so much to say, Richard, and I dare say nothing at all. Listen, my dear. *Paul is dangerous*. I think, if he could, he would kill you – to whom he owes his throne. You must not come to the Lessing Strasse even by night. I think you should leave the country as soon as you can."

"I cannot leave you like this, Leonie."

"Till Wednesday, dear. That is the day of the funeral. Do you remember where we stopped near Elsa and looked out the way to Vogue?"

"Yes, Leonie."

"Will you be there on Wednesday at midnight?"

"I shall count the hours, Leonie."

"Goodbye, my darling," she whispered.

I bowed and stepped back.

A moment later she and Madame Dresden were out of the suite.

Miserably enough, I made my way back to George.

There was nothing to be done. As plain as though she had said it, I read the truth. Prince Paul suspected our relation *and I had made him powerful to find us out.* Yesterday he dared give no order outside his house: today he was almighty. Eager to prove its fealty, every sort of creature was hanging upon his lips. There was nothing to be done.

Three quarters of an hour dragged by.

Then the sergeant-footman came hastening to say that Sully hoped we would come to the dining-room.

The Lord President tried to thank us, with tears running down his cheeks, and, when we begged him to say nothing, he shook his head.

"You do not know," he insisted, "what you have done. Prince Paul will be a focus for loyalty – nothing more. The Council will rule this country, rule it well and truly for years to come. Johann would have been ruthless. In six months he would have destroyed the labour of twenty years. And you have laid the terror – the ghost which has ridden my slumbers ever since Duke Charles renounced his right to the throne."

" 'Cast your bread upon the waters'," said George. "If you hadn't taught us German, and taught us so devilish well, we couldn't have stayed the course. Fancy bickering with Grimm in English as to who was to man which door."

"Listen," said I. "We must go."

"You must see the Prince," said Sully. "He – "

"On no account," said I. "I could give you a dozen reasons, but one's enough. I was rather hasty this morning – at half past three. But one thing you must wangle."

George took out the warrant and gave it into his hand. "That's a warrant for our arrest. They nearly had us on Friday, and – "

"What rubbish is this?" cried Sully.

"Johann's," said I. "Mark that. Johann's rubbish. But he chose his deponents well."

With that, I turned over the sheet and showed him Duke Paul's deposition at the foot of the page.

"My God!" said Sully. He lowered the papers and looked from me to Hanbury with parted lips. "And, knowing this, you – "

"He was only a cat's-paw," said George. "And what we've done, we've done for you and my lady – don't forget that. By the way, tell me one thing. I know why you were so anxious to – to save his throne. *But why was she?* I mean..."

Sully put a hand to his eyes.

"God forgive me," he said, "but I can think of no reason why she should have raised a finger in his behalf. She – she is a great lady."

George returned to the warrant.

"Perhaps you can get hold of Weber. The simplest way would be to have us policed. If we could have a man attached to us – to tell his unenlightened comrades to let us alone... I mean, we'll be leaving today."

"It shall be done," said Sully. "A man shall be sent to meet you in a quarter of an hour. But you cannot go like this. When the funeral is over – "

"We shall not leave Austria," I said. "We'll have a weekend together, as soon as you have the time."

Here Kneller came in, to say that Sully was needed to deal with some matter of State, but he would not go until he had seen Bell and Rowley and had thanked them in the name of the country for what they had done.

Kneller was very civil, but seemed very much relieved to learn that we were leaving the country without delay.

"It was highly irregular," he said, tugging his heavy moustache. "I never thought to subscribe to such goings on. I am for rules and precedents, and you – you have driven a coach and six through the lot."

"True enough, sir," said George. "But at a critical moment you took the reins."

For the first time I saw the man smile. Then, as though to correct such a lapse, he put up his eye-glass and drew his brows into a frown.

"I trust," he said roughly, "I trust your men are discreet."

"They are ex-soldiers, sir," said George.

Kneller nodded approvingly, and, the moment seeming propitious, we took our leave.

Our parting with Grimm was less simple.

The old sergeant-footman was at a loss for words, and, now that the strain was over, our recent, curious relation troubled him as never before. He begged us to forgive him if he had seemed disrespectful and thanked us a thousand times for making his path so smooth, and at last, to our great distress, he began to weep, declaring that his master 'now in heaven' would remember our devotion and would intercede with St Peter in our behalf.

Then nothing would do but we must enter the bedroom and view the dead Prince, "for," said he, "it was you, sirs, that brought him his peace at the last. On Saturday morning I gave him to understand that four strong men had been sent to see justice done, and thereafter he fretted no more."

So once again that day we looked upon the face of the Prince, whose livery we had been wearing, whose name we had never heard a fortnight before.

Then for the last time we used the passage, and thirty minutes later we were back in our flat.

Once there, we wasted no time.

A car was procured, and Rowley left with the detective to fetch the Rolls. We had no sooner bathed and changed than they were back, and, before the clocks had struck two, our baggage was at the station and we were over the border and were taking the Salzburg road.

I think it was natural that the next three days should hang most dull and heavy upon our souls.

Indeed, to me life seemed to have snapped off short, and, when I awoke on Monday, to find myself at Salzburg and to see the dormers of the houses against our old inn, for a moment the waters of dejection passed over my head.

The Grand Duchess apart, the burden of the last ten days had been so strange and brilliant that our simple habits of fishing sequestered streamlets and proving the countryside seemed to us jailbirds' portion and our very freedom a prison into which we had been suddenly cast.

But for George Hanbury, I think that I should have done nothing but wander the streets of Salzburg, wrapped in melancholy and staring at every clock, but, though we came nearer to a quarrel than ever before, he insisted that we should go fishing and put our minds to the business of finding unmapped waters and beguiling suspicious trout. Whilst I was still protesting, he called for Bell and Rowley and bade them have the Rolls ready in half an hour, and, ere they were gone, began to go over our tackle as though some throne were depending upon whether we caught any fish.

So we went forth that Monday, as though Vigil was a phantom city and all our late adventure a lively dream; and, though for the first few hours our occupation seemed hollow and our surroundings strange, the sights and sounds of the country soon came to refresh our senses and our simple pastime in some sort to fill the blank.

For all that, I cannot pretend that, after the business of king-making, the tempting of sprightly fishes was anything but very small beer, and, while it was honest medicine and did us a world of good, the hours went by very slowly and life seemed uneventful and monstrous smooth.

We did not speak of my lady, for, for my part, my heart was too full, and George had no comfort to offer that was not cold: but I fancy he thought of her often, and I know that never for one instant was she out of my mind.

As I have said, at the moment that I knew that I loved her, my world was changed: and, when I learned that she loved me, my world was changed again. Our love for one another preoccupied my wits, and all that I thought and did was subject to that desperate condition which Fate had brought about. To pray to be delivered never entered my head. I would have fought like a madman to keep my yoke. Yet this was very grievous and like to grow more heavy than I could bear.

The future appalled me.

Prince Paul's jealousy apart, no fellowship was to be thought of, if only because I could not stand it – and that was the simple truth.

I would build her the house I had promised, but not whilst she lay at Littai, three miles away. I would see her, if this could be compassed, from time to time. But bear her company I dared not, because I loved her too well.

Yet my world without her was bleak as a winter's day, and I knew that only her presence would ever lighten the darkness in which I was now to dwell.

So much for myself.

Of what lay before my darling I scarcely could bear to think. I was at least a free man. I need take no wife to my wounding, to mimic her lovely manners or ape the brush of her lips. But she – she was to go in marriage to a man as vile of body as he was vile of soul.

The shocking thought that by my interference I had not only bound her more straitly to this her unhappy fate, but had bruised her heart, which, but perhaps for my coming, might have been always whole, sent me half out of my mind. At such times, cowardly enough, I fled back to my own misfortune, to scourge myself with the terror of my long drive back from Elsa and of taking up the thread of a life which had been very happy and was now to be very sad.

Shakespeare has said somewhere that 'men have died and worms have eaten them – but not for love': and, though I am a child in such matters, I cannot doubt that he is right. Even in those three days I never doubted it. But, though I was not to die, Leonie, Grand Duchess of Riechtenburg, was a maid whom once a man had laid eyes on he never forgot. Her physical beauty was so startling, her nature stood out so handsome and all her ways were so royal that, had she not lived so lonely and out of touch, I think she would have been the darling of half the world. And I was in love with this nonsuch – and she had come to love me. I do not think I should have been human, if her loss had not promised to be an abiding sorrow.

At eleven o'clock on Wednesday I brought the Rolls to rest at the spot where, six nights before, we had looked out the way to Cromlec and on to Vogue.

Only Bell was with me, and I think he knew as well as I did that I was to meet the Grand Duchess – and take my leave.

The night was superb. A fine moon was sailing low down in a cloudless sky, and the breeze which had risen to temper the heat of the day had sunk to rest. Not a breath stirred the leaves of the chestnuts which hereabouts grew very thick and threw all the road into shadow for half a mile.

I was glad of this darkness and bade Bell put out the lights, and so sat thinking and smoking until it seemed to me that my pipe had gone out.

The silence was absolute, and when an owl cried from some thicket, his lusty sentence had the world to itself.

So for some fifty minutes. Then I heard a car, coming from Elsa, a little way off.

At once I turned on our side lights and stepped down into the road, but, though I expected every instant the lights of the other to appear, I saw no sign of them, and, when I listened again, I could hear the engine no more.

Now I was sure of my place, so I bade Bell stay where he was and strolled down the road towards Elsa, with my ears pricked and my eyes searching the darkness for any sign of approach.

I had meant to walk to the bend round which I had been waiting for the lights of the car to appear, and I had gone nearly so far, when I saw the Grand Duchess before me in the midst of the way.

"I walked on," she said simply. "I told the chauffeur to follow in a quarter of an hour."

As once before, I was speechless, but I put her hand to my lips.

I lifted my head to find her eyes upon me, and then she was close in my arms and my cheek against hers.

"My darling," she breathed, "my Richard, if I had not seen you do it, I would not have believed it could be done."

"It was your wish, Leonie."

"I cried for the moon, and you gave it into my hand."

"We were very lucky," said I. "And Kneller – "

"Who gave him his lead? Whose courage stung him to action for very shame?"

"We will not argue it," said I. "You were always out of my reach, and I have set a gulf between us which can never be bridged." I let her go there and covered my eyes. "I deserve no better. That night, here, where we are standing, Fate played clean into my hands, and I was so gallant and cunning that I could not see my fortune, but threw it away."

"Richard, dear, it would have been no fortune to take a renegade wife."

"Not if she was to be unhappy. But, anyway, the thing is done." I stood up and drew a deep breath. "We were to build your lodge, dear. If you will send word to Jameson, I should like to begin at once. All of us need distraction, and – and it will help me, my darling, to try to set up your home."

"You are very sweet to remember – "

I cried out at that, as I think any man would have done. Then I put my arms about her and held her close.

"Don't say I may not do it," I said. "We will go about it quietly, and, if you will tell me the way there, no one in Littai need know. We will not use the village. But let me do you this service. Oh, Leonie, my darling, don't stop me – it's all I've got."

She put up a hand there and touched my hair.

"I am going to Littai, Richard. I…"

My heart gave one mighty bound and then stood still.

Her perfume was in my nostrils, and her eager breath upon my cheek, and she was shaking a little, because my arms about her were quivering, do what I would.

"So be it," I said hoarsely. "I will wait until you are gone."

"Why so, my darling? In my own village – "

"Because I cannot stand it," I cried. "Because I love you too much. Things have gone too far for me. I cannot be your neighbour…because I have kissed your lips."

I bowed my head, and she put her arms round my neck.

"I loved you," she said gently, "before you loved me. That day in the courtyard at Anger, when you stared, and I lost my temper, and you – you brought me low. I loved you then, Richard. And, perhaps because I am a woman, I knew that you would come to love me…"

"Well, something had to be done. Either I must see you no more – or else I must be free to come to you when you spoke.

The point was how to be free. I could, of course, have turned down Paul there and then. I had only to go to the Prince and decline to marry a coward, and the Prince himself would have told me to go in peace. I say, I could have done so, and yet... I could not. I had been chosen for Princess, as you may well believe, against my will: and *the man who was to bring me that honour* stood in peril of losing his throne. His ship was sinking, Richard, and the rats were leaving it – leaving it right and left... I have my faults, my darling, but I am not a rat. More. I am Leonie of Riechtenburg. Of her it must never be breathed that she had thrown over a man *because he could not bring her the honour which she had been led to expect.*

"So, you see, there was nothing for it. Either I must see you no more, or – or *Johann had to be beaten and Paul proclaimed.*"

My ears were singing, and my darling's face was all misty, three inches away. I tried to speak and could not. Instead, I began to tremble from head to foot.

"This day I broke off my engagement. Sully and Marya were present. The news will be made public a week from today."

Still I could say no word. Only, for me the heaven seemed to have been opened, and the silence filled with music and the darkness with light.

"Oh, my dear, you do not blame me for keeping you in the dark? You do see that I could not tell you? I could beg you to help me, but I could not tell you the reason why Paul's accession meant to me more than life."

I could only cry over her name.

"Leonie, Leonie."

"More than life, my darling. And you – you brought it about."

Now, when she said this, and I saw by what a hair's breadth our sorrow had been turned into joy, a thrill of fear ran through me. And that, for some strange reason, brought into focus my most astounding fortune, so that for the first time I saw it clearly and knew that I was not dreaming, but that Leonie, Grand Duchess of Riechtenburg, was to become my wife.

"I – I came to say 'Goodbye'," I faltered. "I thought perhaps I should never see you again. And now…"

"What now, Richard?"

"I am very happy," I whispered. "I am so very happy that I do not think I have ever been happy before. I – I have no words, my darling. And, if I had, I could not say them, because my heart is too full."

I felt her clasp tighten, and I think that she understood.

Presently she drew down my head and kissed my lips…

In the distance an engine was started. Then a car began to approach.

As in a dream, I loosed her and began to walk by her side, not looking where I was going, but staring at the slim, white fingers that lay on my sleeve.

"Sully and Marya are here. They have come to say 'Goodbye' and to wish us good luck. And then will you drive me to Littai? My great-aunt is there. And tomorrow perhaps you and Mr Hanbury will come to stay. And if you do not mind a poor lodging and if you can – can stand me as your neighbour for two or three weeks…"

What else she said I do not know and of the meeting which followed I have no clear recollection, save that Marya Dresden was weeping and Sully was deeply moved. But they were both very cordial and spoke most handsomely, and the Countess kissed me at parting, because, I think, she did not want me to find her tears unfriendly to the choice the Grand Duchess had made.

And then we were in the Rolls and were driving for Littai as we had driven for Anger a week before.

There is little more to be told.

Though my marriage must end our alliance, that finest of friends, George Hanbury, rejoiced with me. Indeed, my splendid fortune might have been his, so gay and debonair was his company and so gracious and lively his wit.

Beneath his blithe direction the rebuilding of the lodge became a festive business. The work was after our heart, and Bell and Rowley took to the enterprise, as children let out of school.

Six weeks we played with our toy – with my darling, bright-eyed, in our midst; and Sully came twice to see us and Marya Dresden three times. Then we set our faces to England, and the future and all that it held.

My lady we left in Paris, to follow in ten days' time, and so came back to Maintenance as we had gone. This on a beautiful evening, just as the rooks were homing and adding to the peace of sundown by their ancient and comfortable cries.

Of my parting with George I find it most hard to write.

It had always been agreed between us that he that should first marry should take the place; there was, therefore, no argument, but it shook me to see the packing and disposal of George's things.

He had made up his mind, however, to live in Town, and so was content to leave some stuff and his hunters and, after a struggle, to promise to hunt from no other house. This meant that we should constantly see him for some five months of the year, and I do not believe a man's word was ever more gladly given or more joyfully received.

And so it happens that we sit down to dinner as often three as two and that Bell and his old companion still clean our tops together and share their memories.

So much for the friends that did fully as much as I did to win me my beautiful wife – of whom herself I will say nothing, but that I find her, as ever, the finest lady in the world.

Our life is quiet and simple, for that is the life we love, and the tumult of those wild ten days seems to us to grow more monstrous with the passing of time. This, I think, is natural; for from first to last we were fighting a losing battle and the hopelessness of our venture rode, like a hag, upon our nerves –

yet, but for our holding on, Leonie Chandos would never have graced our table or ridden to hounds in the English countryside.

When I think of this, I fall silent, as well I may, and the scenes of our great endeavour take on a significance so dreadful that I strive to put them out of my mind. Sometimes they will not be denied, but gape upon me, like the Psalmist's bulls of Basan, until, one after another, I look them down.

I hear the slam of the tempest upon the Rolls and the shocking roar of Grieg's pistol behind my back: I see Barabbas looming in the twilight and the bailiff's sinister figure on the bench by the door; I smell the choking reek of *The Square of Carpet*, and I hear the clatter of the shutter which George let fall; I see the quiet Lessing Strasse and the faces of the policemen beside me and the second car storming towards us with open doors: I see the royal apartments and young Grimm watching the telltale, and I hear the sentries spring to attention a foot away: I see the Grand Duchess in the wardrobe and us all, like sheep before the shearer, dumb before the doom of her words, and I see Johann lolling and smiling and the desperate, hunted look upon Sully's face...

As I review these matters, so surely they lose their sting and come to seem no more than the clouds which gather to wait the rising sun: and, to be honest, if I were given the chance of wiping them out of my memory, I know in my heart that I would not let them go.

DORNFORD YATES

AS BERRY AND I WERE SAYING

Reprinted four times in three months, this semi-autobiographical novel takes the form of a conversation between members of the Pleydell family; in particular Berry, recalling his childhood and Oxford days, and Boy, who describes his time at the Bar. Darker and less frivolous than some of Yates' earlier books, he described it as 'my own memoir put into the mouths of Berry and Boy', and at the time of publication it already had a nostalgic feel. A hit with the public and a 'scrapbook of the Edwardian age as it was seen by the upper-middle classes'.

BERRY AND CO.

This collection of short stories featuring 'Berry' Pleydell and his chaotic entourage established Dornford Yates' reputation as one of the best comic writers of his generation and made him hugely popular. The German caricatures in the book carried such a sting that when France was invaded in 1939 Yates, who was living near the Pyrenees, was put on the wanted list and had to flee.

DORNFORD YATES

BLIND CORNER

This is Yates' first thriller: a tautly plotted page-turner featuring the crime-busting adventures of suave Richard Chandos. Chandos is thrown out of Oxford for 'beating up some Communists', and on return from vacation in Biarritz he witnesses a murder. Teaming up at his London club with friend Jonathan Mansel, a stratagem is devised to catch the killer.

The novel has equally compelling sequels: *Blood Royal, An Eye For a Tooth, Fire Below* and *Perishable Goods*.

AN EYE FOR A TOOTH

On the way home from Germany after having captured Axel the Red's treasure, dapper Jonathan Mansel happens upon a corpse in the road, that of an Englishman. There ensues a gripping tale of adventure and vengeance of a rather gentlemanly kind. On publication this novel was such a hit that it was reprinted six times in its first year, and assured Yates' huge popularity. A classic Richard Chandos thriller, which can be read alone or as part of a series including *Blind Corner, Blood Royal, Fire Below* and *Perishable Goods*.

DORNFORD YATES

FIRE BELOW

Richard Chandos makes a welcome return in this classic adventure story. Suave and decadent, he leads his friends into forbidden territory to rescue a kidnapped (and very attractive) young widow. Yates gives us a highly dramatic, almost operatic, plot and unforgettably vivid characters.

A tale in the traditional mould, and a companion novel to *Blind Corner, Blood Royal, Perishable Goods* and *An Eye For a Tooth*.

PERISHABLE GOODS

Classic Yates, this novel featuring the suave Richard Chandos was reprinted three times within the first month of publication, was warmly received by the critics and served hugely to expand the author's already large readership. Typically deft, pacey and amusing, it 'contains every crime in the calendar and a heart-rending finale' (A J Smithers).

A companion novel to *Blind Corner, Blood Royal, An Eye For a Tooth* and *Fire Below*. Gripping stuff.